DALTON'S KISS BOOK 2

KATHI S. BARTON

World Castle Publishing, LLC
Pensacola, Florida
Copyright © Kathi S. Barton 2020
Paperback ISBN: 9781953271228
eBook ISBN: 9781953271235
First Edition World Castle Publishing, LLC, October 5, 2020
http://www.worldcastlepublishing.com
Licensing Notes
Cover: Karen Fuller
Editor: Maxine Bringenberg

Chapter 1

Lizzy opened her eyes. She knew the time of day as well as she did her own name. It was evening. The sun was now behind the hills where she was, and soon the moon would be high in the sky. Giving herself a few minutes to feel sorry for herself, she wallowed in self-pity for the things that had been done to her. Things that she wished daily she could end. But the only way to end her misery was to end her life. That, she thought, was becoming a better idea daily. Being turned into a vampire against her will had been a nightmare for her.

Getting up, she changed her clothing into something warmer. The cave she'd been staying in was chillier than the outside. She was able to change her clothing at will, to be comfortable with whatever was going on beyond the doorway to her own private hell.

Being able to do different things now that she had whatever it was that came with being a vampire had saved her on more than one occasion. Not just the ability to change her clothing, but she'd also discovered, quite by accident, that she could pull a kind of cloak around her and be hidden from people.

When she'd woken up in this very cave eleven months ago, she'd been naked and bleeding from wounds all over her body—bite marks, deep puncture wounds that looked like she'd been stabbed. When she was able to gather her wits about her, she saw the carnage that was in the cave with her.

Six bodies were around the big cave with her, all of them female, and every one of them with the same wounds she had on herself. None of them were alive either. Lizzy had no idea what had happened. It hadn't been something she'd been able to remember even after all this time. However, it was her responsibility to make sure someone found the bodies and that their families knew they had died. She only wished every day that she had been one of the victims.

Taking each of the bodies out hadn't been nearly as difficult as she thought it should have been. Back then, she'd not realized she was a vampire yet. It had taken her most of two entire nights to take them out. She didn't want to get caught dragging them out, so she'd thought nighttime would be a better time to do it.

Having the sun burn her badly the first time she stepped out into the sunlight had clued her in to the fact that something was wrong with her. While her heart worked on what *might* be wrong with her, her stupid head had told her she was a living dead person. A night creature. Vampire. A fucking bloodsucker.

Going out into the night, the veil of the night calmed something in her so deeply that she staggered under the weight of it. It had never happened like this before. The night was welcoming her like a strong man would welcome her into his arms. Moving out into the deeply wooded area to see what had caused such a feeling to wash over her, she felt the rain, gentle drops falling on her face. Lifting up her face, she enjoyed the first normal thing that had happened to her in almost a year.

The darkness of the forest didn't bother her as it might have before all this. She had been, rightfully so, terrified of the dark. Even at twenty-four, she had a nightlight on in her room and one in the bathroom. When she was little, the overhead light had to be on, or she'd wake up in a panic.

As she moved through the forest, taking note of the trees that were changing, Lizzy thought of the night she'd been out with her friends. The last night, as it turned out, of her seeing the sunrise and the moon setting. The day before she was to be married to Josh Hinkley.

She and her few friends had been at her bachelorette party. It was nothing more than dinner with her three closest friends and very little drinking. Lizzy never had been a person that drank much. That night was no different. However, as the night had worn on, she got sick, so sick that she was in the bathroom when someone called an ambulance. After that, everything had become a blur.

"Miss." Stopping and turning slowly, she looked around. There wasn't anyone around that she could see. Pulling the shield around her, she stood very still. "You've been out and about for the last few months now, and I was wondering if we could, I don't know, become friends. I know that our kind and yours aren't friendly, but you seem so sad."

"What do you mean, my kind? What are you?" He told her. "I don't—I started to say I don't believe in faeries, but then I never thought there were vampires either. Just what I read in romance books. Where are you?"

He said his name was Hal, the little person appeared just as she let go of the shield around her. When she put out her hand, he landed in her palm and sat down. The two of them stared at each other for several seconds until he smiled at her. Lizzy asked him why he thought he'd want to be friends with her.

"As I said, you seem so lonely. I am as well since my mate passed away." He moved to stand on her shoulder, and she moved deeper into the forest to the pool of water she'd found earlier in the summer. "The pond that you use, miss. You're very careful of not disturbing the plants and such. That's what made me think you'd be a nice vampire. Not like some of those others."

"I take it you know a lot of vampires." He said he had to know them, to avoid them. "Yes, well, I wish I had been better at avoiding them. The one that did this to me, he did it while I was out with some friends."

"You didn't give him permission?" Lizzy told him she'd not even known he was around. "Yes, they're tricky like that, they are. But to make you one of his babies? Well, that's against the law of their kind. You should tell someone."

"Who would that be? Is there some sort of lawyer that represents vampires that have been changed like I have?" He said there was one they all answered to. She laughed a little. "Not that it matters now anyway. I killed him a few months ago. He came back, I guess, to see how many of us lived."

"You killed a vampire? My goodness. I've never heard of such a thing. You must be strong." She didn't comment. While Lizzy was stronger, she didn't think that was what he meant. "There is a vampire you are required to report to. Just to let him know you're around and that you're not going to do any harm to anyone. You've not done that, have you?"

"I don't know a lot of things I should be doing. Is there a rule book or something I can check out at the library?" After explaining to him what a library would be, he told her he didn't think they'd have a true book on vampires. "Of course they wouldn't. Why would they? Most people don't believe in them anyway."

She was at the pond when he moved to sit on one of the stones nearby. Lizzy had been careful of what she did here. Not having any soap was all right, she supposed. But what she wouldn't give for a bar of it, and some shampoo.

She'd have to take care of that the next time she went into town.

As she stripped down, she spoke to Hal. "The morning I woke up, I found myself with a lot of dead women. I found all their purses so I could write down their names. No one has found them yet—I checked just yesterday. But it's sad for me to know their families might be missing them." She stepped into the water, not caring at all what Hal thought of her being so free with her nudity. He asked her about her family. "Mine has been gone for a long time now. I never knew my mother—she died long before I was able to remember her. I've no idea who my father was. My memories are only of me being in an orphanage until I was old enough to get out on my own."

"I'm sorry for that. I have plenty of family, but they're all busy and working. I was retired, you see." She nodded as she washed her face with the cold water. "Would you like for me to do anything for you? I can do most anything so long as it's not to get me into trouble."

"I'm all right. I don't socialize anymore. Not that I did that much anyway, but now that I'm forced to be alone, I don't mind it much." She thought about her house but knew that it would be dangerous for her. "The cave has all that I need for now. I don't know what I'll do in the winter months again. It was terribly cold last winter."

Lizzy thought of the fire she'd been able to make, the things she'd been able to get sent to her. Having money had saved her a great deal of heartache, and a lot of trouble she might well have had if she'd been broke. Every day she was happy for the fact that she'd gone to see her attorney a few days after she figured out she'd been turned into a vampire.

"You thinking of going to see the vampire I was telling you about?" Lizzy dressed herself in a pair of jeans and a heavy sweatshirt, her usual mode of dress. She asked him if it was necessary. "It is. He is a good man, ruler of so many, but he doesn't like rule-breakers. Shall I make you an appointment time to see him?"

"Why do I need an appointment to see him? I mean, is he really that busy?" Hal told her he wasn't sure. "I'll go and see him tonight if he can work me in. Otherwise, he'll have to wait for a few days. I'm going to see about looking up the man I was supposed to marry. He's not been at his house for some time now."

"You do know you can't be taking vengeance against humans." She asked him why not, not that she was planning on it. "I just wanted you to know that. You did say you're not sure of the rules of being what you are."

"Thank you. Where is this man? The vampire? If he tries to hurt me, I will be pissed off. I've had enough shit going on in my new life that I don't need someone else doing things to me that I have no control over." He said he didn't know the man, but he had heard good things about him. "Then would you please go and see if I can talk to him tonight? I've got to get going to see Josh. He'll need to know what is going on."

It never occurred to her that he might still wish to marry her. She didn't think he had it in him to marry someone different than him. Not that they had had a great deal in common in the first place. Marrying him was just an act of convenience on her part. He professed his love to her, many times, but she'd never been able to tell him she loved him because she didn't want to start out their life together with lies. Now that it was over. Lizzy thought she was happy with that turn of events.

When Hal left her, she made her way to the graves of the other women. Two of them were younger than her. All of them had been redheads and thin. She wondered, often enough, to put the question to paper if the vampire had been looking for them to be the same or if it was just a coincidence. Not, as she had told Hal, that it mattered now. The vampire was dead.

They were all still there, all of them with their purses hanging on the makeshift markers she'd made them. It occurred to her when she was putting them in the earth that she might have left enough DNA that someone would be looking for her. Lizzy thought she'd welcome going to prison and to be put to death. Living like this wasn't anything that she wanted in life.

Sitting near the graves, she spoke to the women as she did every time she came to see about them. She told them about Hal and that he was taking her to see a vampire in charge. Picking a piece of the beautiful fall foliage up from the ground, Lizzy's heart broke for them.

"I'll make sure you're found. It's all I can think about. Your families must be heartbroken to not know anything. I hope you have no children that miss you. I think that would be hardest of all to know." She knew nothing of the women other than what was on their driver's license. "I surely wish it had been any of you that had lived. I welcome the thought of ending my life daily. Hourly, actually. I'm so sorry this happened to you."

Hal joined her a little while later. Sitting upon her knee, he told her that the vampire wasn't far from here and was awaiting her to come to see him. Standing up, she followed the little person out of the dark woods and into a large open area that looked to be under construction. Not caring what was being built, she didn't bother reading any of the signage but looked for the vehicle that was to pick her up.

"He's a better man than I'd been told about." She nodded. For such a little person, he could certainly fill in the spaces of quiet time. "His missus, she's a hoot, I tell you. There were times when I thought she was the leader instead of the mister. She has a nice way about her, but I think she's bossy about things. Told me I was going to have to eat something before I was to leave. I've never been treated so by a vampire."

"What is it you eat?" He named off, she would swear, every flower in the world. Not just that, but he told her the season in which each was in its best bloom. There was no need for her to acknowledge that she'd heard him either, for he never paused in his speaking.

When they were at a crossroads in a smallish town, she sat down on the sidewalk and let the soft rain fall upon her again. "Is it true I can never get ill again?"

"It is." She stood up and backed away from the large man that had spoken. "My name is Bancroft Dalton. My wife, Kelly, is here with me so you won't be afraid."

"I'm not afraid." She wasn't either. For whatever reason, she didn't feel anything at all toward this man. "Why don't we just talk here? I don't need to go with you to wherever you wanted."

"It's my home. And I believe it is necessary. Hal said you were changed against your will. I'd like to get some answers from you about that." Lizzy told him the vampire was dead now. "Yes, he told me that as well. That should be something we discuss. How a baby vamp could kill an older vampire."

Not having much of choice, she got into the long limo with him. His wife, Kelly, told her that she was there so she'd not be too frightened. She told her what she'd told the man, she wasn't afraid at all.

"He thinks everyone is going to be terrified of him when they find out he's a vampire. I was, too, I guess you could say. But I didn't let him bully me around." Kelly smiled at her. "I don't think you'd be bullied around much now that I've met you. How did you kill the other man? Did you have to stake him through the heart?"

"No, I ripped his throat out when he tried to strangle

me. Apparently, him making me do what he wanted wasn't working, and he called me a broken victim. I didn't know that meant he was going to kill me. So I killed him before he killed me." Kelly asked her if he'd used compulsion on her. "That and his fists. I didn't actually know he was trying to use the first on me until he held me above his head with his fucking fingers around my neck. He called me broken. I showed him what broken was like to fuck with me."

Bancroft laughed, and she looked out the window. It might have been funny to people now, but it hadn't been for her. Lizzy had been afraid of dying. She had no idea why, when she would welcome it so readily now. But she supposed they'd get to that before she was released to go back to the cave.

~*~

Remy put the phone back in the cradle. He didn't so much want to toss it across the room, but to tear the wall out and then find the man he'd been talking to. No one, it seemed, could find the man who had been telling the vampire league he'd been making baby vampires.

"We're back."

He smiled. Remy had only been here for a week now, and he was already in love with Kelly Dalton. Banny had hit the jackpot where mates were considered. She was fun, loving, and had a heart of gold. She could also keep Banny from going over the deep end when things didn't turn out the way he wanted them to.

"Remy, come and meet our new houseguest."

"I think I made it perfectly clear that I wasn't going to be staying here, Mrs. Dalton. I have a place to say." If Kelly answered her, Remy didn't hear it. "I know you're my boss of sorts, but I'm also my own boss. Who do you think I'm going to listen to more? I'm going to tell you you're wrong if you think, once again, that it's you."

Banny came into the room he was in, smiling and shaking his head. Remy asked him what was going on. Still smiling, he sat down in the chair across from the desk he'd been using and laughed a little before speaking.

"This woman was changed against her will and hasn't the first clue about rules regarding being a vamp. Yet she is stubborn as all get out. Kelly is frustrated with her if you can believe that. My little wife is being told no by a vampire less than a year old." His look was serious then. "Whoever changed her managed to kill six other women at the same time. She's the only one that survived. In addition to that, she's been living alone, in a cave, without anyone to help her out. She told us she's not bitten anyone and plans on never doing that. Elizabeth Strickland—she goes by Lizzy—has been feeding off rats since she woke up. Oh, and she killed her maker because she could ignore his compulsion. Remy, either she is a natural-born leader, or she's been changed by a powerful vampire. She's stronger than any newborn I've ever encountered."

"Do you know who it was that did it?" Banny said she wouldn't allow him to figure it out. "Won't allow you?

What sort of messed up shit is that, Banny? I told you I could stay someplace else, and you ordered me to keep my ass here." They were both laughing.

"Seriously, Remy. She's strong enough to keep me from ordering her to do things. I could really push it, but I don't think either of us will come out unscathed from it. There is something about her that worries me. Not about her, but whoever this person is that changed her. If there was that powerful of a vampire in my area, why did I not ever feel it?" Remy could tell he was worried. And like he said, not about the woman, but this other vampire. "the one she killed might not be the one that changed her. I asked her about the night she was changed, and I checked—there are no memories of what happened to her at all. Like—"

"Like someone erased her memories." Banny nodded. "Why? Why do that to someone? Especially if your plans were to kill her all along. I can't believe for a moment that this person changed her only to decide to kill her. Also, how, as a baby, could she push off compulsion? Something isn't right here."

"Why? Because you weren't there to witness it? That you'd do something differently?" Both he and Banny stood up when the woman spoke from the doorway. Kelly was right there with the woman, and she too was spitting mad. "Is it because the great and powerful vampire men are so astonished that a woman such as myself could take care of herself? That's it, isn't it?"

"I'm sorry. I didn't mean for you to overhear us." Lizzy,

Remy thought Banny had called the woman, snorted at them both. "You were the one that was eavesdropping. What you heard was two old vampires speculating on why you were changed and left for dead as the others had been."

"So you're speculating that I killed them? Is that your conclusion? That since I'm a baby vamp, I'd have no ability to be able to do anything but be a killer." Remy started to tell her that wasn't what he meant. "I've had plenty of time to come to terms with what I can do, mister. I'm sure this will tie your knickers up too."

He felt himself being lifted from the floor and then slammed hard against the ceiling. She did it three times before he simply dropped to the floor. Before he was able to stand, she picked him up again, holding him up by magic and one leg as she moved toward him. He could see the anger on her face then. It was like a shield of armor he might well have worn long ago.

"I'm sorry." She told him to fuck off. "No, I'm truly sorry that I misjudged you at all. You're stronger than any of us thought."

"Oh, so now you have it in your head to kill me off too." He shook his head, but she was pissed and going to do him harm. "Killing me isn't going to be as easy as changing me. I'm telling you exactly what I told the monster that changed me when he came back to the cave to collect what was left of us. He actually was thrilled to tell me what he'd done to me. I'm awake now, and full of whatever fucking shit he did to me."

Remy was blasted across the room. This time he hit the wall hard enough that he was unconscious for several seconds. When he opened his eyes, he saw Banny stand up, as if he was going to tackle the young woman. Before he could move, Banny was bound to the chair he had been in without any ropes or chains. Remy couldn't move either, only to watch Lizzy walk to the desk and put down a sheet of paper.

"These are the names of the other women. There are markers where they are buried, as well as their belongings in their bags hanging from the markers." She turned to both of them again. "You come near me again, and I won't hesitate to try and kill you both. I know you're stronger, I can taste it. But at this point in my fucked up life, don't expect me to fight back. The sooner I can end this shit, the better off I'll be."

Then, just like that, she was gone. Disappeared as if she'd never been in the room with them at all. Remy stood up, checking to make sure he wasn't bleeding out anyplace he'd not be able to fix. Banny could now move too. His body wasn't nearly as beaten as Remy's was, but he had the look of something that had been tangled with. But instead of being as pissed off as Remy was, Banny started laughing. It was a good five minutes before he could slow enough to speak.

"We've just gotten our collectives asses handed to us by a newborn, Remy. Not only that, but she could have killed us both, I think, and not thought another thing about it." Kelly asked Banny if he was sure. "Yes. She had me hogtied to that chair, and it would have been nothing for her to take out my throat. With Remy, she could have slammed him against a chair—I have no doubt about her aim being that good—and it would have killed him too if a chunk of wood ended up through his heart. She's not one to mess with. I would hate to be around when she finds the person she's mated to. Christ, there is no telling what sort of magic she'll have when she's found him."

"You two should be beaten." They both looked at Kelly, and Banny said he was sorry. "Sorry isn't going to cut it. Do you have any idea what she's had to endure? To find not only that she was something else, but that she's literally left her fiancé at the altar? To wake alone in a cave filled with the bodies of others like her? To have to bury them all by herself? What do you think would have happened if that had been one of you? Do you think you could have done so well for yourself? I don't think so. Lizzy told me she had no idea what was wrong with her when she woke up, naked and bleeding all over her body. That there wasn't a note, nothing for her to go on for the date or how long she'd been in there. The first time she thought she knew what she was was when she stepped into the sunlight and nearly died, a whole month after waking. I'm ashamed of both of you. Ashamed, I tell you."

She stormed out of the room, then came back in. Neither of them knew what was going to happen until she slapped them both. Remy felt the pain of the slap all the way to his feet. Not that she'd hurt him, but that he'd driven her to do it. He liked the younger woman.

"You two are going to stay away from her. Do you hear me?" They both said they would. "What do you think your parents would say if they saw the way you acted today? I know, they'd be appalled. Just as I am. What do you think your grandmother is going to say, Bancroft? I'm sure she's going to be thrilled to death that she wasn't here to witness the great Bancroft getting his bottom handed to him by a mere slip of a woman."

Neither of them moved when she left them the second time. When they were sure she wasn't returning again, Banny sat down in his desk chair and held his head up by his hands. Remy thought for sure he was sobbing until he lifted his head, and Remy saw that he was laughing. He asked him what the hell was so funny.

"Not once, but twice today we've been put in our place by women. What do you think your parents would have said about that?" Remy laughed and said they'd tell him to marry her. "No doubt. She's strong-willed, Lizzy is. Heaven help us if she's a mate to anyone we know. There isn't any way that she'll be forgiving us anytime too soon. Now that she's a vampire too, she might well outlive both of us."

After a few more laughs, the two of them spoke about the call he'd gotten and how he'd been trying to trace the man who had been telling the league lies about him.

Kelly had been helping him with his receipts for paying his dues. Hopefully, she'd still help him out with that. But now, well, he just didn't know. He had managed to piss her off as well.

"What is this vampire's name that is accusing you of making baby vamps?" Remy told Banny it was all there in the paperwork that had been sent to him. He told him his name too. "Calhoun Richardson isn't a very common name, do you think? I mean, not in our world. We're both lucky that we have family that goes back for generations, or we might not have adopted a last name. But Richardson doesn't ring any bells with me either."

Jamison had been walking by the door when they were talking. He paused in front of the doorway and asked what they were talking about. He'd not meant to be rude, but he just wanted to know why they were discussing Richardson.

"You know him?" Jamison told Banny that he'd heard the young lady mention his name as her maker. "Are you sure? I mean, you're sure that's what she said his name was?"

"Quite sure, sir. She said that Cal Richardson was the—pardon my language—but the bastard that had killed her. I do believe she was telling the young miss that she was ready to meet her own maker now that he was out of commission. Does that mean she wishes herself dead, sir?" Remy answered for Banny. "Oh my. That would be a terrible shame. The lady of the house was quite taken with Ms. Strickland. I do now remember seeing her name some time ago in the newspaper. Not long ago. I do believe, if he is the one, this might help Lord Remy with his predicaments with the league."

Jamison walked away, telling them he was sorry for interrupting their talk, and Remy looked at Banny. It couldn't be the same person. His luck was never that good. While Banny tapped around on his keyboard, Remy had to think if she'd mentioned the vampire's name. Thinking that he had to find her, he decided he might well live longer if he went to see Kelly. She was pissed at him too, but he wasn't nearly as afraid of her as he was Lizzy right now. She'd already wounded him once, his pride and body. Remy thought he'd be less beaten up, at least physically, if he groveled to Kelly a little.

Before he left the office, Banny told him he'd found her name in the paper. "Remy, she was set to marry a man by the name of Josh Hinkley. You don't know him, do you?" Remy went to the computer when Banny turned it in his direction, laughing. "Boy, talk about it being a small world. She was created by your accuser, Richardson, who is blaming you for making baby vamps. She was going to marry a man by the name of Josh Hinkley, an ass of the highest order. She certainly might be strong, but she has nasty taste in men. There is an entire article here that tells what sort of ass Hinkley is."

Remy read the article about the wedding that wasn't to be. He also saw where it mentioned Lizzy had disappeared with six other women the night of her bachelorette party. It was speculated then that Josh had done something to his bride to be. However, since her attorney had been in contact with Lizzy in the months following her disappearance, there was nothing they could pin on him about the other missing women.

Chapter 2

Josh answered the phone on the fourth ring. He didn't care for the telephone, but he was trying to find out who Lizzy's attorney was so he could have a little talk with him. It would be like Lizzy not to be dead. He'd been planning her demise for months before she'd been kidnapped, or whatever had happened to her. But he'd been planning for it to happen after they were married. She had herself a nice little nest egg built up that he wanted in the worst kind of way.

"Josh Hinkley here." There wasn't a sound on the other end of the call. "Hello? This is your dime, so speak or stop calling me. I'm a very busy man."

Still nothing. He started to hang up when he heard someone speaking. Josh pushed the phone harder to his ear, trying to understand what was being said. He didn't think whoever it was, was speaking to him, but he needed some answers and thought this caller might have them.

"Did you say this was Josh Hinkley?" He said that he

did. The woman's voice was one he'd never heard before, but he knew instinctively that she was calling him for a good reason. "I'm calling you from Parker Insurance. The policy you have taken out on Ms. Strickland has been denied payment. There is evidence she is still alive, and the policy is going to be canceled as well. For reasons of trying to collect on a living person, if you'd like to know."

"How do you know she's alive? Have you seen her? I've not. She hasn't been seen since the night before we were to be married. If she is dead and I can prove it, are you going to pay off then?" She told him no. That was all, just a simple no. "And the reason for that is what?"

"The policy states that you were wed, and you are not. The premiums were to be paid monthly, and you've missed several payments. There are a list of other reasons why the policy has been cancelled, and they are being mailed to you with the policy marked as denied. You have a good day, sir." He told her to wait a moment. "I'm sorry, Mr. Hinkley, there is nothing more that we can do for you. Also, we've notified other agencies that you are trying to collect on the death benefits of a living person. I'm sure if you've taken out more insurance on Ms. Strickland, those too will be cancelled. You have a good day, sir."

This time she simply hung up on him. Damn it all to hell and back, he needed that money. He wished he'd killed her himself now. All he had to show for dating the damned woman was a ring he'd gone into great debt for in hopes of making Lizzy trust him more. The engraving she'd wanted on it was why he couldn't return it. Fuckity fuck, he was beginning to hate everyone.

He hadn't wanted to marry Lizzy. She didn't love him, and he certainly didn't love her. When he'd asked, he hadn't expected her to say yes. Well, it was more like an "I guess so" than a yes. But the money she had in the bank and her job made him think they could work it out to his advantage until he found someone else. What he hadn't expected, however, was to find out a week after she left him at the altar that she didn't just have money in the bank, but had a great deal more than that.

Houses, cars, businesses. She traveled a great deal too. He'd thought she only had a simple job to do and didn't spend her paychecks on silly, girly things. That had been a sore spot a couple of times when they'd gone out. He thought she should be willing to pay for meals since she was working. Lizzy pointed out that she'd not wanted to go out in the first place, so he should pay. After that, they rarely went anywhere except to her home or his apartment.

Josh realized about a month before the wedding that she wasn't going to be as free with her money as he'd hoped. Asking her if she'd put him on her accounts, she flat out told him no. Then, when he asked her to help him out with his rent that month, she refused that as well. The next night, she sat him down and told him, *if* they married, there were going to be rules.

"What do you mean *if* we're married? I thought with the invitations going out tomorrow that things were set for us." She explained to him about her money. "What about *us* having the money? Sharing the bills and even paying off credit cards. I'm sure you have enough to take care of all our bills. Mine can go for extras."

"I don't mind paying half the bills we incur as a couple. However, I'm not going to pay off things that you had before we got married. Nor would I expect you to pay mine if I had any. I'm not a sap, Josh." He was so dumbfounded by her reasoning that he just sat there. "Now that we have that out in the open, I'm not going to put you on any of my accounts. You're a man with means, right? I mean, you seem to have money in your wallet all the time. If you want any extras, as you call them, you can use your money after the bills are paid. Also, since I'm assuming we'll live in my home, half of what the house payment will be is part of your bills. That's only fair since I'm paying the taxes and upkeep on it."

"It sounds as if you don't trust me with your money." She said she didn't. "Why not? I mean, it's not like I'd make you broke. That would be stupid of me, don't you think?"

"It would be stupid. Something that I'm not." She got up, making her way to the dining room, and came back with a sheet of paper. Handing it to him, she sat down on the couch across from him. "In the year that we've been seeing each other, you've had a total of eleven jobs. That's a job you've lost per month, Josh. Also, you've had your car repossessed. From what I've found out about you, you're four months behind in your rent. You're currently unemployed, and you waste your money on odds at the race track, as well as football games. As you mentioned, the invitations should be going out tomorrow. However, I'm not going to send them out until you have a job. I'm not a sap, as I said. Taking you as my partner in life means that we both will give our all to being married. You can't, in your current state, even buy a newspaper to look up any listed jobs."

They'd had a vicious fight. Josh had tried to hit her a couple of times, but she'd been able to knock him on his ass instead. When the police showed up, about ten minutes after she'd bloodied his nose, he was told to leave, and she didn't make sure he was all right. After that, he'd tried his best to make it up to her. Josh even told her he had a job. He did, just not one she would approve of.

The invitations, as far as he knew, had never been sent. The more he thought about them, he didn't think she'd ever had them made. The day before they were to be wed, that afternoon, they'd had a second fight, and this one had sent her for stitches and him spending a few hours in a cell. At least until she had made arrangements for him to be released around midnight. Much too late, he thought, for him to have been able to talk to her again. Then she was gone.

He had hired a man to knock her around a little. That was all. The fact that she was missing from everywhere had bothered him enough to find the guy. He said that since he'd never seen a dime of the money Josh had promised him, he'd decided not to engage with Lizzy. Like they were going out on the town or something. So where the fuck was she?

No one seemed to be too worried about her being missing, really. Her attorney, Josh supposed, was making sure things were taken care of with her job and shit. There hadn't been any article in the paper, but her name was attached to several other women that had gone missing that night.

He'd read the article that had been in the paper several days after he'd shown up at the courthouse to be married. No one knew anything about a wedding to take place, and that had pissed him off royally. Nor did anyone have any idea what he was talking about when he told them he was to have his name on all her accounts.

Josh knew it was a long shot to lie his way into her accounts. Hell, it was the least she could have done since she'd not married him. But that was locked up tighter than her legs had been when he wanted to screw her. She had this unthinkable idea that they should wait until they were married. Bitch. That never happened either.

Now, here he sat, waiting for her to come home at some point so he could have a very long talk with her about scheduling and showing up on time. Of course, he didn't have a job as she'd told him. Nor did he have a place to live. The landlord had kicked him out just yesterday when he'd been unable to come up with six months of past due rent.

"Everyone is out to get me." Josh didn't really think that. He knew he was a fool and was lazy. That's why he wanted to marry someone that would take care of him in the manner in which he wanted. Thinking he had that in Lizzy was what got him into trouble in the first place. Secondly, he thought she never had any intention of marrying him at all. Lizzy was just trying to make him part of the working class like she was.

"I don't want to get a job. Nor do I think if she has one, I should have to." The house that he was sitting by, her house, was locked to him as well. He'd been here before, of course. However, there had never been staff running around. Nor had he been able to venture any further than the kitchen and living room when he was there for the evening. Now there was a man at the gate who demanded he have some sort of prior arrangements to see the lady of the house before he was able to breach the high electrified gate. Finding that out a little too late had his hand still burning from trying to scale it.

"Mr. Hinkley, it's time for you to move on. I've called the police and—" He asked him what he was doing that he'd have to call the police. "You're trespassing, for starters. There is no way we're going to allow you on the property until we hear differently from Miss Lizzy. Also, you should know that if you are to gain access—which I can't see happening—but if you do, we're going to shoot you. No warning shots either. Just pull out a gun and shoot you where your brain is supposed to be residing."

"Are you fucking me? You'd shoot a man when he's trying to see the woman he's marrying?" The guard, dressed in camouflage and a heavy-duty vest, told him she didn't marry him, and it didn't look like she was going to. "How the hell do you know? For all you know, she might be planning a bigger wedding than before."

"Well then, if that's the case, I'm truly sorry. But until we all hear differently from her about keeping you off any property that she owns, then you're just shit out of luck. I have my orders, and those are to keep you out of her home. Her home, not yours and hers." Josh stood up, trying to make himself look larger than the man in front of him. "Mr. Hinkley, I'm only going to say this to you one time. You don't want to fuck with me. I'm bigger, meaner, and a good deal smarter than you are. Now, move along before they have to come out and put your body in a bag to get you out of my hair."

He started walking back toward town. The police pulled up behind him and kept pace with him as he took his time walking. They even turned on the siren when he paused for too long. It was the lights that got him pissy. Why did they have to announce to the world that he wasn't welcome someplace? Fuckers. Everyone was a fucker today. As he walked, Josh started thinking of all the names he was going to call Lizzy when she showed up. If she showed up.

"Where the hell are you, damn it?" He didn't expect an answer, but he surely would like to have one. She'd been gone now for a year, and he was no closer to talking her into marrying him than he'd been before. "I wonder if she'll even consider me now. Probably not."

Laughing at his own little joke, he was nearly run over when the cop car went around him and sped off with all their sounds and lights. He didn't know what was going on, but they sure were in a hurry. Josh started to pick up his pace but figured he'd have a heart attack out here, and no one would give a damn, so he walked on into the town to see what all the hoopla was about.

~*~

"What the hell did you do to me?" Bancroft was confused and looked to Kelly when Lizzy smacked him in the chest and yelled at him. "You had to do something to me. I have all this extra shit going on, and I can't fucking control it."

"Perhaps if you would calm down a moment, we can get to the bottom of his. What extra crapola do you have?" Bancroft was used to Kelly not cursing, but when Lizzy looked at her oddly, he felt the need to explain. But Kelly started talking again. "Why don't you have a seat, and we'll see what it is that has you upset. Please?"

"What planet are you from? Crapola? Is that even a word?" Lizzy glanced at him, then looked back at Kelly. "I have this extra shit. Like I can fucking move through the walls of where I'm staying. The rock walls of the cave I'm sleeping in."

"I'm assuming you weren't able to do that before. All

right. Let me see if you can explain to us why you think my husband had anything to do with it." Lizzy sat down, and she looked upset. "I can't help you, Lizzy, if you don't try and tell me what you mean. I'm better with information than I am at just having someone accuse me of something."

"I didn't accuse you, but him." Lizzy pointed at him. "He's supposed to be this big assed vampire that everyone in the world has to talk to. Why? I have no idea. It's like a lot of other shit I don't understand."

"I can help you with some of it. Bancroft gave me a book you can read to see what things you might well be able to do. Now, what else can you do? I'm assuming from your tone that there is more than just teleporting through walls." Lizzy asked Kelly if she was always this calm. "Most of the time, yes. Flying off the handle, like some people I know, doesn't get you much in the way of information."

"You mean like me." Kelly shrugged. Bancroft figured he could sit down now and not be smacked around again. He and Kelly had been coming into town for the pumpkin show being held at the grade school. "I went back to my place after leaving your house, and Hal was there. He said something about me glowing. I thought he meant he could see how p...ticked off I was and ignored him. But then later, when I was looking at one of the walls in the cave, I saw this spot of gold. I thought, what the heck, I can work on seeing how big this is. You know, having something to do through the long night. I frigging went into the wall and came out with a hunk of gold as big as my flipping head."

"Oh, what a wonderful find. You must be very happy with that. I don't know the price of gold, but to—" Lizzy told her to keep on track. "Yes, of course. All right. You can go through a wall of stone and find gold rocks. What else? That couldn't have been all of it. I mean, you seem very upset for just one thing."

Lizzy stood up and looked around. Putting out her hand, she had a ball of flame in her palm. Not only a flame but one that was white-hot and actually shaped like a ball. Tossing it up in the air, she touched it as it was coming down, and the thing separated into small sparkles of light that danced around the table they were sitting at.

"That's very lovely." Kelly looked at him then. "What would you have done to her to have caused such a phenomenon to happen? I mean, who else would it have been? You remember when I first met you, you only had to walk into the door, and I was tossed back with some sort of magic stuff. Could you have given it to her too?"

He was beginning to see the big picture here. Shaking his head, he looked at Lizzy, then back at Kelly when she said his name. Kelly asked him if he had it figured out.

"I think so. You're not going not like my answer any more than you did, thinking I did this to you." Lizzy asked him what he was talking about. "The only other person in the house with us, the only other person that could have given you more magic, is more than likely your mate.

Remy was with us when you came to the house."

"You think that Remy is her mate? Oh, how wonderful. Remy will be— I was going to say he'd be thrilled, but I don't think he will be, will he?" Bancroft shook his head at his wife. "Yes, well, he'll just have to get over it. He and Lizzy will make a fantastic couple. I think—"

"I'm sitting right here. And if you think I'm going to be a mate to some other vampire, you're more insane than the man who did this to me. I'm not long for this world. I promise you, if he comes sniffing around, I'm going to stake him. No kidding, either." Kelly told her she couldn't hurt her mate. "Well, isn't that just fucking great? Yes, I said fucking. I'm not going to dance around with my curse words just because you're old fashioned."

Bancroft reached out for his friend. It was nearly nine-thirty now, and he figured he'd be finished with the paperwork that had to be filled out with his supposed non-payment of dues. He told him what he'd been discussing with Lizzy and how she was taking it.

What the hell do you mean, you think she's my mate? I don't know if you realize this or not, but that's not how that works. I find her, not you find her for me. He told him what she'd been doing since he'd met her yesterday. Remy was quiet for some minutes before he spoke again. *I think you might be right. Banny, not only have I gotten a bit more magic since yesterday, but I'm also feeling less stressed. Where are you?*

He told him. *However, I'm not sure you should be coming around. There are a lot of people here that will see her kicking your ass when you confirm she's your mate.* Remy laughed. It was the first time he'd heard him laugh in ages. *She also told us she's going to end her life. It's not the first time she's said that. I would normally think she was all talk, but she also told Kelly yesterday she promised that the women that were with her when she woke up would be found. Kelly is going to find them tomorrow. I think that is the only reason she's not let the sun take her by now.*

I have to speak to her, Banny. If for no other reason than to confirm that we're mates. I don't need one right now either, but if she is my mate, and I've no reason to doubt that she's not, then if she goes, so do I. Does she understand that? Banny pointed out that she knew next to nothing about being a vampire. *Yes, I guess she'd be against it anyway. Don't you think?*

They both laughed. Remy said he'd come to town. He did need to talk to her before the league took him away for non-payment of dues. He told him he'd see him in a few minutes. Bancroft looked at Lizzy when he realized he might have missed something she and Kelly were talking about.

"You told him, didn't you? You just had to go and start flapping your lips and tell on me. What the hell is wrong with you? Is it a vampire thing or something? That it's impossible for you to keep something that doesn't concern you at all to yourself?" She got up and started pacing. Bancroft realized she paced like she talked, hard and without mercy to anything that might be under her shoes. "I have so much shit going on right now that I don't think I can handle one more thing. The idiot I was going to marry is trying his best to make sure I'm dead so he can collect on the insurance he took out on me. I'm also pretty sure he hired someone to kill me off after we were married. Then, the company I've been wanting to purchase for over a year is wanting to sell now. How the hell do I get to a meeting in the morning when I'm going to fry myself just thinking about it? I have a faerie too, one that simply talks all the time and asks more questions than anyone I've ever known before. However, he is nice to me. Other than the fact that it was his fault that I had to go and see the big bad vampire that can't keep his mouth shut."

"Are you finished?" She turned and looked at Remy when he joined them. "I don't want to interrupt you while you're on a tirade. But there are a couple of things you should know. First of all, yes, you are my mate. I should have realized it the other day when I was here. Also, and this is very important, I won't demand anything of you. Not now, not ever. I know better. I think too that if this other man that thinks he's going to marry you shows up, I can just sit back and let you handle him. You've shown yourself capable of taking care of yourself, even against all odds. I do hope you know you were very lucky to have survived being changed."

"I don't want to be a vampire." Remy told her she'd have to get over that; it was done. "I can kill myself. I just wanted those women found."

"That's bullshit, and you know it." Kelly came and

sat closer to him. He was glad for it. Lizzy looked deadly enough to take him on too. "Why do you care if those women are found or not? For that matter, you could have called the police and told them where they are and joined them. You wouldn't have been found, however. But then, as I was able to find out, you don't have any family anyway."

"You don't know shit." Remy sat down and asked her, politely, to sit with him. "I don't want to sit with you. I want to go back to where I've been staying and let you get on with whatever you have going on."

"I don't have anything going on just yet. I do have some things I need to take care of. Mostly vampire shit. But for now, I think the two of us should get to know each other before we come to blows. Tell me about this guy that thinks he's going to marry you." She asked him why he'd want to know. "Because I need to know if I need to make arrangements to have an alibi when I kill him. I'm a very possessive vampire, as most are, but with you, I think I can let you handle most of the dirty work while I bask in your beauty."

"Don't be cute. It doesn't suit you." Bancroft saw a hint of a smile before she stiffened again. "I was changed against my will. I know nothing about your kind or what I'm supposed to do now that I'm a night creature. I'm depressed most of the time, terrified that I'm going to lose control and bite someone. I don't want to bite a person. I can't make myself think about it without being ill."

"You won't be able to feed from anything but me from now on. I'm to understand that you've been feeding on rats and other rodents. That will no longer fill you. I'm sorry. Neither will I be able to feed from someone else." She glared at him. "If you don't believe me, ask Banny. He knows that rule. Also, and this is a biggy. If you were to meet the sun as you've been saying, I will as well. Now that we've met, if I don't feed from you or can't be near you, I will turn rogue and have to be put down. As in, I will turn wild and kill whatever I happen to be near, or be killed."

"That's the stupidest thing I've ever heard. What happens if I just get killed by some random shithead? Does that mean you'll have to die too?" He said it did because he could not live without her love. "I don't love you. I don't know if I ever will. As a matter of fact, I don't have any idea how to love someone. I've been alone for all my life, and I like it that way."

"I've been around a great deal longer than you have, and I also have been alone for most of it. My parents are both dead. They were killed when I was just a small boy. If not for Banny here, I would have been killed along with them." She looked at him, then back at Remy when he spoke again. "Also, and this is just a theory on my part, but I have a feeling that because the two of us are mated, and you're already so strong, you have more of my traits than you think. Such as, I'm betting you can stand the sun where you wouldn't have been able to before."

"I can be out during the day?" He could hear the longing in her voice. It hurt him, seriously put a pang in his heart, that she'd missed something so profoundly as having the sun on her face. "That alone would make me want to be your mate. You have no idea how much I've missed having the sun on my body when I go running."

"I'm not positive about that one, but it's easy enough to figure out. Also, you won't have to feed so much now that you're my mate. You've discovered you have more magic already, so that's good."

They were still sitting there when Kelly pulled Bancroft up from the table and led him away. They'd either work it out or not. However, Bancroft had a feeling they were well on their way to getting their lives together. Bancroft hoped with all his heart that this would help them both. They needed each other more than he thought he did Kelly. And he needed her with every breath he took.

Chapter 3

Remy didn't join her in her cave but sat outside when she went into it. He wasn't pushing his luck with her. He thought she might well hurt him, rules or not, simply because she was jumpy enough without him stirring her up again.

They'd talked well into the night. He had wanted to stay out with her to see if she could indeed see the sun, but he could tell that she was afraid — not of the sun, but of her not being able to see it. Take one step at a time, he told himself. If he didn't, he might find himself out in the sun with a long stake in his heart.

Hal came out of the cave just as the sun was peeking through the trees. Remy lifted his head up to the bright lights and realized he couldn't remember the last time he'd enjoyed such a thing. The sun was something he'd missed too when he'd first changed. Now he wanted to spend as much time as he could feeling it on his face.

"She's awake. Pacing. She does that very well, you

know." He told Hal he'd seen her doing it last night. "Yes. Well, I think should she stay here forever, she'd wear a nice long trench in the stone. I'm to ask you if you think she can come out."

"Yes. If nothing happens, she'll be fine. If it does, I am here to help her save herself. Is she upset?" Hal said she was, but he thought it was more to do with the phone call she got when she woke. "Is everything all right?"

"Don't know. She seems to be upset about everything all the time. I don't think it's in her nature, but she has been tossed a great deal of late. Miss Kelly is coming to find the bodies this morning. I do hope my lady can be there with her. It will make her feel much better, I believe." Remy said he thought it might too. "May I ask you a question, sir?"

"Anytime, Hal. But don't expect me to butter coat something for you. If you ask me, like I think Lizzy does, I'm going to give you the answer truthfully." He nodded as if he'd been told that before. "What is it you want to know?"

"The miss, she was powerful in her own right. Did you know that?" He said he had figured that out, yes. "We, the faeries and I, we think she was powerful even before she was changed into what she is now. Long before you came along, and the other vampire."

"What is it you're trying very hard to tell me without upsetting me?" Hal looked at the opening of the cave, then back at him. "Hal, just tell me. I don't care to have my information in half sentences any more than I like to give it out."

"We think she might have been part vampire before she was changed." Remy thought about that and thought Hal might be on the right track. "She's not taking it well, but her magic, it is surpassing anything she should have had. Before you, we mean."

"Who is the we you're referring to?" He told him. "I had no idea that you were having trouble with the other faeries, Hal. If you want, I can talk to them. Do they know what a fine job you're doing with my mate here? You should bring them around some time to meet Lizzy. I'm sure Lizzy would enjoy that very much."

His chest puffed out, and the strain on his buttons was very noticeable. A faerie worked hard all the time, but like any creature, they enjoyed a compliment as much as the next person. Hal seemed to be taking his to the top.

"What would Lizzy like to do?" Remy stood up and saw that she was just inside the cave where the shadows were still darkest. "I'm sick with worry that this isn't going to work. I know I shouldn't get my hopes up that far, but I already have."

"Come out and see." She stood there, and he could see that she wanted desperately to do it. Instead of telling her to come out, he tempted her with things she'd be able to do when it worked. "I'm betting you have a house that you miss, too, don't you? Not to mention, you said something about a company you wished to purchase. I wanted to tell you this yesterday, but it slipped my mind. I have a great deal of money. I've been around for a very long time, and I didn't have much use for things such as stoves and air conditioning. So I invested wisely."

Remy had no idea if she was going to be able to be out in the sun, but he had a feeling. A feeling so strong, he wanted to lift her up toward the sun and let her feel it over her entire body.

She put her hand into his when he held it out to her. He could take on the world in that moment. Not just take it on, but conquer the entire universe if she would allow him to hold only her hand for the rest of his days. As soon as she stepped out into the sunlight, he moved back so she could see it all. Feel the warmth of it that he vowed never to take for granted again.

"It doesn't burn." Her laughter rang through the woods like a waterfall that fell from hundreds of feet only to splash loudly into the water below. It was a wonderful sound. One that he was going to work every day to hear. "Oh, Remy, it's heavenly, isn't it? The sun isn't burning me."

He and Hal both watched her dance through the sparkling sunbeams. The dew on the grass made her clothing wet, yet she didn't seem to mind. Each time she knocked a few droplets of it off a leaf, the sun would make it all the more beautiful by catching it at the right moment. Remy laughed with her, enjoying something he'd not thought of in a thousand years or more.

"Oh, the things I can do now. Hal told me I'd have to be in when the sun was at its hottest, and I'm all right with that. Just so long as I can feel it on my face once a day, I think I could live forever." Hal started to tell her she would, but Remy stopped him. "I can go home now. Have a hot shower, and even sleep in my bed. To have a real bed and mattress beneath me sounds so wonderful right now. Oh, Remy, this is the best thing that has ever happened to me."

She was still dancing around when Kelly and Bancroft—he was trying to remember to call his long time friend that—joined them. Kelly joined Lizzy, having a grand time with not just the sun, but the feel of a warm flower. A stone that skipped smoothly across the pond.

He glanced at Bancroft when he said his name. He didn't want to hear anything terrible right now and told him that.

"Nothing terrible. I promise. The league is looking into your receipts. Kelly gave them hell, in her own way, when they asked her if she had the originals. They wanted them as well. They don't know, but they might well have destroyed them, and that would have been the last straw." Remy thanked him as he watched the two women. "Also, and you might well get a kick out of this. The vampire that changed her was an old vampire with plenty of magic to keep him going. He had amassed a fortune in cash. They're going to divide it up between the victims that were with Lizzy when she killed him. She's not going to have to pay any restitution either. It was justified as far as we're concerned."

"And his magic? What happened to that? I'm sure someone thought of it." He said he'd brought it up to them. "And does that mean she's going to get that as well? Or has she gotten it already? Could that be the reason she's so strong?"

"Neither of you will get it until you bond. They—we all figured she'd be strong enough after that so she could handle it. There is a great deal of it too, from what I understand. But for as strong as she is now, neither of you will likely notice when it comes to you." Remy nodded and asked when he was going to tell her. "I'm not. You are. She doesn't like me at all, remember?"

"She currently is only tolerating me because she can be in the sun." They both laughed. "What happens after we bond? I'm only hoping we do that someday, but I'm not going to pressure her. I honestly think she'd hurt me if I tried."

"I have no doubt she would. Seriously too. Here you go." He handed him an envelope. Remy snapped his fingers, and the paperwork was magically put on his desk at home. "That is a list of the things she will get from his estate. It's a great deal of money, gems, as well as three houses we've found. She'll get the hard things, the houses, and gems. The rest will be divided between the women's families. There is also an award coming to her for killing him. Richardson has been a black mark for vampires for some time, I heard."

"The magic, do you also have a list of that?" He said he was working on that for him. "Good. Thank you for your help in this. I have made sure that this Hinkley person is kept away from her. After the things she was telling us yesterday, I put a man on him last night. He sounds like a money hungry prick."

"He is. She has it too. Money, I mean. As a matter of fact, she's about as close to you in having it all, as I am. Lizzy is smart and has a good head on her shoulders. She also makes sure that a lot of the charities she donates to have all they need. However, you should also be aware that she doesn't abide by them fucking with the money. If she finds out a charity is using the money wrong, she cuts them off without a second thought." He asked his friend how she made her money. "Investments mostly, but she also won the lottery several years ago. No one ever knew it was her. She kept working at her dishwashing job until they were able to afford to replace her. I've spoken to her attorney, and he seems to think she's about the only multi-million dollar winner that has doubled their winnings within a year, as well as going on to make more each year since."

"Just curious, does this count the vamp's money too?" Bancroft only shook his head while smiling. "Yes, I thought that was what you were going to say. Christ, no wonder that Hinkley guy wanted to marry her and then kill her. She's a catch. Too bad he's going to be shit out of luck."

The women joined them as they set out for the bodies. Remy listened to what Kelly was telling Lizzy, mostly about her job and what she did for the FBI. He'd known that, of course, but not that Kelly only worked for them. Neither of them had to work, but Remy understood that to not work was paramount to getting into trouble. Idle hands and all that.

As soon as they were within a hundred yards of the graves, he could smell them. He glanced at Lizzy when she came to stand with him. It was Bancroft that explained why the smell was still there after all this time.

"You see, when you buried them here, they couldn't decompose. Their maker, even though they were killed, wasn't the one that buried them. By you doing it, and it was great that you did, they could only completely become one with the earth after he was killed. It's why when a vampire changes someone, and they die, they burn the body. It's the only way to make sure they're not found by someone that can pull them from the ground." Lizzy told him that it was weird. "Yes, I agree. Once you killed Richardson, not only did they start to rot, they also had no blood in their bodies. There won't be any wounds on them to indicate how they were killed. The only thing Kelly will be able to tell about them is that they were dead for however long it's been since Richardson was killed. They were young and female. There will be no obvious signs of trauma to them at all."

"So how does she tell someone they died? Someone is

going to want to know a reason that all six of these women are dead and buried together. I'm sure their families are going to want to know the truth." Bancroft told Lizzy that they would be considered homicides because there would be lies printed on their death certificates. "Then how will anyone know that their killer has been disposed of? I mean, I would love to have killed him and had a body to go with theirs, but he turned to ash the moment I tore his throat out."

Remy cleared his throat before he explained what would happen. "There are people in place in government offices and the like that work with our kind all the time. Changing the name of a property that we might have owned for several generations. Things like that. After a couple of months, no longer than that, I'll call one of the offices and tell them the killer has been found and killed. There will be a small article in the newspaper. The families will be given a great deal of cash, and it will soothe them knowing the killer has been caught." Lizzy told him it wouldn't soothe her. "No, it wouldn't. But you won't have a vampire coming to your home and making you believe everything is all tied up in a neat little bow. It's for the humans, Lizzy. They need this more than any other species the earth holds."

Remy could see she was struggling with the lies of it. He would, too, he supposed if he'd had to live through what she had. And she had too. A great deal of terrible things that should never have been done to her, nor the women that had died that day.

Kelly made two phone calls. First, to the FBI to have the grounds excavated and the bodies removed. Then she called the funeral home in town to let them know what to expect. Her story for finding them was that it was at the back of their property. Which, as of that morning, Kelly told them, it was. She and Bancroft had been out walking and stumbled across them.

"I won't have my name in the paper, nor will any of us for that matter." Lizzy said that was good, but why. "Because I work for the government, and that's part of my deal with them. Also, I think you have to lay low because you have things to take care of first as well. Correct?"

"I do, as a matter of fact." Lizzy looked at him as Kelly spoke to the people she'd had on standby for this. "I need to talk to you about some things. Things that I have going on in my life that you might want to know about."

"I'll be happy to know anything you're willing to tell me." Lizzy told him he might not. "Whatever it is, we can figure it out together. I have things going on as well. We'll get through it. I have a feeling we'll come out on the other side smarter for it too."

"Christ, I hope so. I would hate to think that neither one of us is all that smart." He laughed with her when she guided him to her cave. "I've not just been laying around on rocks here. I've made sure I have all the comforts of home."

Laughing, he nearly fell back when he entered her

cave, as she called it. Good lord, she really was living with the comforts of home. He loved the fact she'd not been sitting idle but had kept working even with her inability to be out in the sun.

~*~

Lizzy looked over the paperwork that had been sent to her from her attorney. Mike Holloway had been working with her since she'd gotten out of college. While he went on to be an attorney, she'd gotten a business degree and had taken a lot of money management classes. He had other clients, but he was there for her whenever she needed him.

"I will say this for Josh. He's persistent. Calling the insurance company daily was what got them looking into other policies. I have a feeling that had you gone through with that marriage, you'd have not been long for this world." She asked him if Josh had been able to collect any money. "No. Even his own accounts are closed off to him. Not by me, though I wish I had been in on it. He's been nagging the banks, saying that since you are gone, he should, as your almost-husband, be able to have half the funds in there. Like I said, he's persistent."

"What can you tell me about Stanley Remy? Not that it matters, according to Bancroft, but is there anything there I should be concerned with?" Mike told her he wasn't an easy man to get to know. "I've noticed that. While he talks to me, I think he'd rather be someplace where he didn't have to interact with people as much as I do."

"He has money in both the local bank as well as out

west. I do believe he has stashes of it all over the world. If he's as old as I'm to believe he is, I'd say he's also a very intelligent man. Both his parents are dead. He hasn't any relatives that he has much to do with. Also, you should be aware that he's put your name on his accounts. I found that out yesterday when I was working on setting up the account you asked for. The money, or whatever comes from your maker's estate, it'll go right into that account." She thanked him. "No, I should thank you. I wouldn't have thought of putting money like that into an account other than your personal one. Who knows what sort of things they might well do to your account with access to it."

"The house—have you had it taken care of?" He told her all the locks had been changed, and there was someone at the guardhouse all day and night. "Good. Kelly gave me a book to read over. It said that in order to keep up appearances, you should have a full-time staff on hand so you could look human. I honestly never thought of myself as anything but a monster. I just never thought I'd ever be able to go back to my place."

"I'm learning a great deal too. Remember that professor we had for literature? Well, come to find out, the reason he's so well versed in that art is that he's been around for a while too. I was just making inquiries into finding someone that would be able to help you, and he was the one that called me back. He doesn't know Remy well, he told me, not enough to form an opinion, but he does know Bancroft." Lizzy asked if he had a good opinion of him.

"He does. Everyone I've spoken to, they say he's a fair man, and since he's found his mate, he's become friendlier, as well as more of a philanthropist. You and he have that in common."

"He's a pain in my ass is what he is. I like Kelly, his mate. She's friendly and charming. The funniest thing about her is that she never curses. I mean, Mike, she uses words like butt and darn it. It's hard not to laugh at her sometimes." Lizzy smiled. "I think Bancroft is afraid of her too. She has that—I don't know what you'd call it, but she can peel your skin right off your body and smile the entire time she's doing it."

"No wonder you like her. You're just like that too. I've never seen a man shiver in his shoes so much as when you're giving him a dressing down. It's funny how you can insult someone, and they're still thinking you're polite as hell." Mike laughed. "My goodness, I think you might fit into this group more than you think."

They worked on the paperwork that had been lying on her desk and his for most of the morning. She knew it would be important for her to take a nap during the hottest part of the day, and she was all right with that. This morning she'd watched the sun crest over the mountains. Lizzy decided she never wanted to miss it again. It was the one thing she'd miss more than anything else.

Lizzy went to find Remy. He'd told her he was going to look her house over to see if it was safe for a vampire to live in. He'd not pushed her into letting him move in with her. Arriving at a decision was difficult. Remy was starting to grow on her, but she didn't want to have to give into him either.

"There are only a few things I'd change out here. It's mostly to do with the bedrooms. Each of them has windows, of course." She asked him if they should be taken out. "No, nothing that drastic. There are darkening curtains you can buy that will do the trick. I'd not put them in all the rooms either if I were you. Just the ones that someone such as yourself would use. If anything, the basement here has a suite in it that would be perfect for a visiting vampire."

"Where are you planning to sleep?" She hadn't meant to ask him, much less ask him like she was accusing him of something. He only smiled at her, and that made her feel more stupid. "I'm sorry. I'm not used to having to share my things. I mean, I guess I should know that you're not the pushy type—you've been so laid back with me. The next time I sound nasty to you, go ahead and be nasty right back."

"I don't think that would make either of us feel better. I know you have a lot of stress in your life. I also know, from your staff, that you're usually not so upset like you are now. I can wait. I'm in no hurry to have you accept me." She asked him what he meant. "Not whatever you're thinking. I mean, just you having me around to help you get through this. It's difficult to ask for help. I know that firsthand. I want you to be comfortable about not just me being here, but with what you are now."

"I don't know what I am." It was the first time she'd said it aloud but still felt the need to explain. "I know I'm a vampire. But what does that mean? Really? What's the big deal about being able to kill someone with a slash of the hand or drinking them to death?"

"You're only focusing on the things that bother you. There are a great many things you can do now that you weren't able to before, one of the most important ones being that you're going to live forever. You'll heal quickly. No more sickness or broken bones that take weeks to heal." She told him she couldn't eat her favorite meals anymore. "But you can. Just not as often as you wish. Having a steak once in a while is perfectly fine. You'll enjoy it as you did before. However, you'll fill up quicker, and it won't satisfy your real hunger."

"You mean for blood." He nodded. "I've never bitten anyone before. I don't think I even did it as a child. I don't know if I can or not."

"I know this sounds contrite, but it's not as bad as you're thinking it is. When you bite me, you'll find that you're— I guess refreshed is the word. Sex is usually involved. A good strong climax can make the blood richer for it, and the taste is like a great wine that is aged to perfection." She cocked her brow at him. Of course, Remy laughed. "You'll have to figure it out on your own, I guess. But it is amazing. Especially between mates."

"Kelly said she can bite Bancroft too." Remy explained to her it was because she was the kiss leader's mate. "I guess I can understand that. What I don't understand, and maybe you know, is why I can do so many things she can't. You're not a leader, are you?"

"I'm not." He asked her to have a seat. They were in the kitchen again now, and she sat down on the stool she'd bought for this room especially. "It has been brought to my attention that you might well be a leader. Also, that there might be a couple of vampires back in your lineage. I know there are ways to check that. As we can't ask your parents, we can do this one of two ways, if you want to know."

"I do. One of them is a blood test, right?" He nodded, then shook his head. "What? Is it or is it not a blood test?"

"Yes, it is. But it's not your standard blood test. If you were to go to a regular doctor to find out information about your blood, there would be too many questions. As vampires rarely get ill, there aren't a great many physicians out there for our kind. There are doctors, but usually, they're human doctors." Lizzy nodded, not at all sure where he was going with this. "An old vampire, such as myself and a few others that I know, can take a small taste of your blood and not only know who your maker was if you have one but if there are any other vampires in your bloodline. All you would get from mine is that I'm from a long line of vampires. There aren't any humans that we've been able to trace back through our lives. The thing too is, we've lived for so long we pretty much know who our line is."

"I don't know why, but I believe you." He thanked her. "No. That's not what I meant. I mean, I believe you when you tell me you can taste my blood and know. That this isn't a way for you to taste me with trickery."

"I wouldn't do that to you. However, if you'd like for Bancroft to do it, he would willingly. Or any of the others we know that are as old as we are. Bancroft's grandmother could also could help you. I don't think you've met her yet." She shook her head. "She's gone to take care of some business deals that needed her attention. Also, that's another thing. We have invested in a great many starter businesses that have gained a great deal of recognition since they started."

"How long will it take you to figure it out?" He told her it would only take a few seconds. "That fast? I thought it would be like a DNA place and be months. All right, will you see what is going on with my blood? I'm honestly not sure I want to know, but I also think it might come in handy. I don't know why, but it could be important. Right?"

"Yes. For children, should you want to have any. If you have much in the way of vampire blood, you could well have a full-blooded vampire child. It will, I guess, be easier for you to conceive too." Lizzy put out her wrist and told him to do it. "There is no turning back from this once I take your blood. I mean, I'll be able to—"

"I know. Even with you knowing my every thought and idea, I just want you to tell me." He leaned over her wrist and licked the pulse there. Her body heated up to about a thousand degrees, and she felt wet. "Christ, just do it."

The bite wasn't anything. There was no pain at all, not even a small pinch like a needle would give a person. When he sat back, his eyes closed, she saw a drop of her blood on his lip. Before she could point it out to him, he licked it. It was by far the most erotic thing she'd ever witnessed.

"I can smell you." He looked at her, his eyes a darker color than the blue they'd been. "You smell like sex. Wet sex that is making it difficult for me to think. Can I kiss you, Lizzy? Just once to see if you taste as good as you smell?"

Chapter 4

His beast was right there on the edge. Remy had never had trouble calming his other half, his beast, but he wanted his mate as much as he did. When Lizzy nodded and slowly moved toward him, Remy picked her up from the chair she was in and sat her on the table as he stood up.

"All you have to tell me is no." Lizzy nodded at him, but he wasn't sure she understood what he was desperately trying to tell her. "I'm going to try my best not to take more than you're offering me. I want the kiss, but the need to roll you back on this table is stronger than I've ever felt before."

"Have you had other mates?" He told her she was his first and only. "Good. I have no idea why I'm saying this, but I truly want you to take me. To fuck me until I can't stand up."

"Christ." He laid her back on the table. When her head touched it, he ripped her clothing off from neck to knees. Remy paused a moment, just long enough to look at the beauty that was laid out before him. "Perfection. Beauty. They seem like such minor words to describe how you look to me."

Lizzy cupped her breasts. At her moan, he lifted her legs up and put them over his shoulders, thinking that if she came a few times, perhaps she'd be readier to take him. Licking her from gate to clit, he realized his mistake. It wasn't her that needed preparing, it was him. He was never going to get beyond tasting her.

Taking a seat in the chair behind him, Remy suckled on her clit as he sat, tasting the heavy warm juices that easily filled his mouth. Each time she moved, every time he licked at her spice, she would make a sound that would make him need more of her. Give him the power to hold off, taking her hard until she was as ready as he could make her.

She came twice, flooding his mouth. When she begged him for more, Remy made sure he held tighter onto her thighs, drinking greedily from her. Anything to distract him from standing up and plowing her where she was.

"Please, Remy. I want to feel you inside of me. I need you to take me." He held on. Making her come three more times gave him the time to back off that he dearly needed. "If you don't take me, I'm going to do it myself."

Her fingers joined his tongue, dancing over her clit. Chasing them, he was able to make her come twice more as she played with herself. It was, he thought, the sexiest thing he'd seen.

When he stood up, he looked at her breasts, pink with need. Her nipples were red from her touch. Remy slid his cock to just her entrance, and she screamed out a climax that pulled him deeper into her, had him breathing hard at just the thought of coming inside of her. Before he could manage to hold off for a few more seconds, Lizzy wrapped her legs around his waist and pulled him tightly against her.

"Fuck me."

He did, nearly tossing her off the table, which moved to the counter across from them. As soon as the table was braced as tightly as it could go, Remy leaned over her again and took first one, then the other breast into his mouth, suckling hard on the tips and feeling his cock fill tightly, his balls curl up against his body, ready to fill her.

Biting down on her nipple filled his mouth with her hot spicy blood. Her tightening around his cock, her release strangled his cock until he couldn't move. Then she came, came with a voracity that nearly took him over too. Fucking her harder, making sure that she came, again and again, Remy slammed forward as hard as he could as he bit her throat.

He knew it was going to be delicious—Remy had had a taste of her already. What he'd not expected was for it to be so dark with magic, good magic, that it made him come again. As her own teeth scraped over his throat, then his shoulder, he begged her to bite him, to drink from him.

"Now, Lizzy. Bite me now."

She hesitated for just a few seconds, a lifetime it felt like for him. But the moment she licked his flesh, he felt the earth shake beneath his feet, his body tremble with it. When she finally sank her teeth into him, Remy screamed around her flesh as the connection between them was made, their bodies and their minds making them one.

The climax they both shared took him over the edge and into a darkness he'd never seen before. He heard Lizzy calling his name, begging him for more. When she cried out, Remy succumbed to the dark place and let his body go. He only hoped Lizzy was safe and unharmed, as he was no longer able to stay conscious.

When he woke, he was lying on the floor with a blanket over him. Remy didn't have any idea how he'd ended up there, but he was glad he was at least covered. Smiling, he dressed himself and sat up. The room took a hard spin that had him lying down again.

"Yes, I should have warned you about that. It took me three tries before I could stand up. Are you all right?" He moved his body around so he could see Lizzy. She had a small mark on her throat, but she looked amazing. "I thought about moving you to the couch, but I didn't want to drop you. I might have, and then where would I have been? I'm nervous."

"Why?" She shrugged, and he smiled at her. "Are you afraid of me? Of what we just did?"

"I don't know. I don't even know if I'd call it being afraid. It's sort of this foreboding feeling, like something terrible is going to happen to take this, you and everything else, away." He told her he was hers forever. "Will you live here with me?"

"Yes. Tell me why you think you're feeling this way. Is it because of the sex?" She grinned at him and told him it was too wonderful to be afraid of that. "I agree with you. I've never felt like this after sex before. For a moment there, I thought you'd killed me."

They both laughed, but he could see that something was still bothering her. He told her things about himself, mostly mundane things. He didn't want to give her more to worry about. Adding to her feelings wasn't anything he wanted to do right now.

"I have to confront a few things before I think I can go on with my life. One of them is Josh. He's not someone I ever loved, but it just seemed right that we should marry. It wasn't until just now, when you were asleep, that I realized he talked me into marriage. Josh is aware that I don't love him, but it was his idea that we marry so our lives would be easier." She laughed. "I don't think being married to him would have been easy. I might well have dodged a bullet there."

"There are people keeping an eye on him to make sure he doesn't get too close to here. Also, I'm aware he's tried to get into your accounts, as well as your businesses. Does that bother you? Him still trying to get into your life?" She told him she knew he couldn't, but it did bother her, just a little. "I can have a talk with him. In fact, it would be my pleasure to do so. I will make him understand that you and I are together now and that he is just going to have to figure out a way to find someone else."

"Would you kill him?" He asked her if that was what she wanted. "No. I mean, if he tries anything, then I don't have a problem with taking his ass out. But just talk to him. Not that I think it'll do much good. He seems to be persistent, Mike told me."

"Mike?" She explained to him who that was. "I haven't had much of a need for an attorney in a long time. I do have some issues going on that I might need one. Would he be able to help me with some of my vampire issues?"

"Yes. He's been talking to a couple of older vampires that we both know. I didn't know either of them were vampires, but they were very helpful in getting information on the guy that changed me. Oh, what did you find out?" It took him a moment to remember what he'd found out. "You aren't telling me because it's bad, right?"

"On the contrary. It's all good. The vampire that changed you is indeed dead. I know you told me that, but your blood tells me that you are the one that killed him. You have vampire in your blood as well. Old blood, it seems. At some point in your life, a vampire by the name of Fergus had a child by his mate, a human by the name of Beth Johnson. Do you recognize the name?"

"Only my mother's. I mean, I never knew my parents. I've been assuming they were both dead since I was just a child. I did know my mother's name, of course, but nothing more." Remy sat up and swayed just a little this time, so he was able to sit instead of lying down. "So what does this mean for me? Or for us? There is an us, isn't there?"

"There is now, yes. We're a mated couple. Bonded, too, as a matter of fact." She nodded, and he asked her what she was thinking. "Other than the vampire blood in your line, is there anything else bothering you?"

"I don't know what to do." He asked her what she wanted to do. "I'm not sure it's that easy. I have so much going on right now that I'm not sure where to begin. I've been gone from my usual life for nearly a year. I've been able to keep up with most of it, but there are meetings I need to attend that, frankly, don't seem as important as they did at one time."

"Is it because of me?" She nodded, then smiled. "I'm sure you didn't mean that as an insult. Tell me what you meant by that. Please?"

"I want to hang out with you. Not every waking moment, but it's like I'm calm now. That when I'm with you, I feel like I have a better handle on everything. And I feel differently about being stressed. It's as if meeting you has simply taken that away. Am I making any sense to you?" He told her he understood completely. "Do you feel relaxed? Not because of the sex, though that really did help. But I mean, do I do anything to you?"

"You are the reason my heart beats. The reason I no longer wish to meet the sun. It's harder for someone my age to end their life, but it can still be done. That feeling, as well as my dread over going to the league for the nonpayment of dues, doesn't, as you said, seem all that important anymore." He felt he could stand up but still had to hold onto something to steady himself. "I'm not sure what made us both so weak, but I'd gladly do it again with you."

"I forgot to mention that Hal came to see me after I woke up. He told me that the coming together of us was felt all over the area. I asked how far reaching it was, but he didn't seem to know that. The earth, he told me, was happy for our union." She shook her head as if to knock some of her thoughts out of her head for a moment. "We have an appointment with his boss. He told me that she could and will answer any questions we might have about us. Hal said she's been watching over us for a long time. Do you know who that might be?"

"No. I mean, a few names come to mind, but no, I don't know who his boss is. Unless he's talking about the Lady of the Earth. She has been around for a lot longer than either Bancroft or I." Lizzy told him she was beginning to believe no human was aware of everything that goes around in the other world. "We like it that way. The less they know about any of us, the safer we are. We liken our safety to the witch hunts of long ago. For a very long time, vampires were killed because they'd gotten a bad name. I'm not saying all vampires are like Bancroft and me, but when a vampire goes bad, it's bad for a great many people."

"Kelly gave me a book to read. I passed it on to Mike

so he could help me if the need arose that I needed an attorney. But it said the best way to avoid death was not to tell anyone what you are. Is it still that bad nowadays? I mean, it seems to me that vampires have been romanticized in books for a long time." Remy asked her if she read those sorts of books. "Not before being turned into one. Then I just found it to be stupid. None of that shit is even remotely true when it comes to being changed. It's not the least bit loving and happy."

"Not the way you were changed, no. But it can be nice when your mate changes you into what he or she is. It's hard on both of them, however — there isn't anything romantic about having your mate covered in blood from head to toe, and the pain one has is shared by the other. It's a process that could also kill one or both of them." He laughed. "Now that I think on it, it's not romantic at all, is it?"

Remy followed Lizzy around the house as they spoke. She was pointing out things that she thought he needed to know. Mostly it was the rooms he'd not ventured into while looking around. These rooms, he discovered, were empty except for a few boxes labeled by months.

"I buy up baby clothing when I can get it, online or at sales. It's a hobby of mine. I don't keep them for myself, but I box them up by sizes, and when someone needs clothing for a baby, I slip it to them. When I was able to get out, I would have this room filled with things to give away. I want to be able to get out and about doing that again." He told her that was a wonderful idea. "Diapers too, when I can get them at a good price. I have come to realize that even if I had every room in this house loaded with diapers, I'd not have nearly enough for people. That's something else I've been slacking on."

"When Bancroft and the others were just wandering around the world, I remember meeting a woman that had supplies much like you do. She'd take them to places where they could be helpful. I would imagine she'd have a room much like this one if she thought it would help people. What else do you do that I can help you with? Because this is something I could really get behind." She told him about buying water cheap and having it delivered. "Yes, great idea. I know Kelly donates bottled water to the school for events. Bancroft said she had all kinds of ideas like that, where she finds things at a great discount and donates them."

"Maybe we should pool our resources." Remy thought that would be a great thing and told her they were going to their home tonight if she wanted. "Bancroft sort of scares me, but nothing like Kelly can. She's much too calm for me. Perhaps, like with you, she is calm because of Bancroft. She told me she works for the FBI."

"Yes. Kelly has all kinds of medical and forensic degrees. She can take a bunch of bones and get a clear picture of not only how the person died, but also a very close replica of the way the person looked when they were alive." They talked about the little boy that had been murdered some months ago. "She not only figured out who the child was but also had a good idea who had murdered him. Kelly will say it was a team effort. However, to hear Bancroft tell the story, you'd think she could run the FBI department all by herself."

"Their love is so tangible, isn't it? I mean, they look at each other with so much love." Remy didn't tell her he loved her that much—she was still dealing with things. "I'd like that someday, I think. To have someone look at me like I'm a banana split with all the trimmings."

He was still laughing about her comparing love to a dessert when he heard from Bancroft. He told him that the vampire committee he was on wanted to meet him today if they could. After asking Lizzy if she had any plans, he told Bancroft he'd be at the empty building on Main Street in twenty minutes. They decided to walk over—the weather had turned warm again—and enjoy the last few days of summer. Fall was only around a week away.

~*~

Of the three men on the committee, she didn't like two of them. Bancroft was the third man, and the verdict was still out on whether or not she liked him. The first man, his name eluded her right now, kept asking for the original receipts that Remy had. Harlen, the other man, just kept staring at her like he was thinking of where to stick his knife.

Bancroft kept saying the same thing over and over. "Stanley Remy has paid his dues." Lizzy had about enough.

"This is getting us nowhere." She had to agree with that statement from Kelly. If they didn't get their heads out of their asses soon, Lizzy was going to have to get up and smack them. They'd been there for nearly an hour, and they hadn't moved beyond wanting his receipts. She nearly laughed when Kelly stood up, and the room became as still as death. "Excuse me. I'm new to all this, but can you tell us why it's important you have his receipts? I want the truth from you, so no messing around with me."

"We want them because anyone can forge a receipt." Kelly said it was just as easy for them to destroy them. Then she told them to tell the truth. "How did you know that was our plan? Did someone leak that?"

She didn't move when Kelly went to the front of the room where Remy was standing. The men, this time, including Bancroft, stood up. Telling them to sit down, Kelly did as well. Then she smiled at the group of them.

"So, you want to destroy his receipts so he'll have to pay you again. Aren't there other vampires out there you can pick on?" Harlen told her they had fifty such vampires on the hook for the same thing. "I see. So this isn't just Remy you're targeting, but a lot of people. Tell me, why do you need the extra money? I mean, it seems to me to have to pay dues to the league is sort of unfair. Why should people pay for the privilege of being a vampire when it wasn't their fault as to how they were born to be one? What is this money supposed to go to anyway?"

"We use it for things we don't have. Things that we

want." Harlen seemed to be pissed off that Kelly was getting answers out of him when he didn't want to tell her. "If I were to pay you some of the money we gather up, would you not tell anyone of our pilfering?"

"Oh, you've gone well beyond pilfering. What you've done is larceny. Grand larceny, as a matter of fact." She shook her head. "Yes, there is only one way to solve this dilemma you've gotten yourself into. It's to hang the two of you. I'm to understand that is the normal way to rid the group of unsavory people like you."

"You can't do that to us!" She asked him why not. "Because you just can't. We don't want to die. We're just having a good time. This job doesn't pay at all. We were just having some fun with it, and it got out of hand."

"So, you're telling me that you not only stole from the vampires in your care, but you've also decided that since you want it, even more money should be yours for the taking. You didn't tell me what the dues are supposed to be used for."

The two men looked at Bancroft, who told them to answer. The compulsion, something Lizzy had only just figured out how to use, was stronger than Kelly's had been. They both answered Kelly at the same time.

"We never were told what it was for."

"It was there for the taking, so we did." Harlen seemed to understand that he was digging himself deeper into whatever pit they'd put themselves in when he looked over at Bancroft. "You're going to kill us, aren't you?"

Bancroft nodded. "I just knew that you being on the board was going to be a bad thing. But we also thought with you having a mate, she'd keep you distracted enough that you'd not notice what we were doing."

"I wouldn't have noticed now if it hadn't been for my mate." Bancroft stood up, stretching his body to at least a foot taller than he was already. "Think of it this way, boys. You've been taken down by a slip of a human."

With a swipe of his hand, both men were gone. Lizzy wasn't sure if he'd killed them or put them somewhere else, but no one spoke as he sat back down at the table, no longer sitting on the end of it. To all that were there—about fifty or more people in the room—he stated that he was the only man in charge and that he wasn't going to be fucked with.

"Today marks the end of paying dues to the league. However, this does not keep you from having to make a yearly donation to help families of our kind that have been destroyed. This money will be put in a trust that will help with children left behind, the rebuilding of a home that might have been destroyed, as well as money for legal fees if they occur and one cannot afford them. This is not a due, but something that all of us might have to fall back on in the future." Someone asked how much it was going to be. "It's a donation, so that would be left up to you. However, I would expect those that can afford it to put in more than the ones that might have a little trouble gathering some spare money."

"What if someone doesn't pay? I mean, I can see that happening if you don't put out an amount." Lizzy looked back at the man who'd asked the question. He didn't look as if he could afford a good coat, much less dues. Lizzy was standing up before she could think through what was on her mind.

"I'm sorry. But can anyone speak at these?" Bancroft introduced her to the group as Remy's new mate. He also explained how she was made. Not understanding why that was important, she said what she had on her mind. "There are two businesses looking for places to put their plants. I'm in the process of purchasing one of the companies now. The other business is simply looking for a place to expand. It will bring more jobs to this area, nearly a thousand when these are finished."

Remy stood up. "What she's trying to tell you is that if finding a job is something that you're having difficulty with, she and I are going to make it a priority that all night creatures have first dibs on the night shift of the jobs." Lizzy wasn't sure how he'd known that but was glad for his help. "In addition to that, there will be other businesses we'll be helping in the area that will hire more of the residents around town."

They both fielded questions about the new plants. One of them was a sheet factory that made high-end sheets for beds that would be shipped out all over the world. The other company, the one they both owned as of yesterday, was a company that made sandals from recycled items such as old tires and composite wood particles. Each of these new businesses was already established and ready to come to the area.

"Excuse me, I have a question." She turned to Bancroft, just knowing he was going to shut her down before she could even start the hiring process. "Will there be discounts for employees? Will there be an outlet for the seconds? The reason I'm asking is, I have several buildings in the downtown area here that could be used for that. I'd think that would be a perfect way for some of the others around town—teenagers and the elderly—to be able to pick up a few extra bucks by working. We can talk about this later if you're in agreement."

Lizzy wasn't sure. She didn't know anything about partners, so she looked at Remy. With a quick kiss on her mouth, he told Bancroft he could horn in on their plans anytime he wished. The room erupted in cheers that made her feel good about what she was doing.

The meeting ended not long afterward. The questions were still coming but in a less formal way. Two of the people that had been in trouble with the dues as Remy had been came to talk to them. It seemed that everyone wanted in on bringing more jobs to the area. She was glad for it.

"When I was first turned, I walked the town at night. I could see where things needed improvement. The things that needed to have a leg up. There are several homes that could use a little boost too." Lizzy had a list on her of all the things she wanted to do to help around town. She read from it. "The addresses are all here, but there are currently three homes that have tarps over them due to leaks. I think we can do better than that. The area where a great many elderly live could use help too. Painting their homes. Mowing their grass. Trimming trees would really help too. There are at least ten houses that heat by wood. With winter coming up, trimming the trees in one area could go a long way in having wood to heat with in another part of town."

Before they were home, she and Remy had been nominated to be in charge of the housing upgrades. There were donations made that would go to helping not just put roofs on some houses, but to put money in the soup kitchen, she'd not known about.

As they traveled to Bancroft's house, she and Kelly made another list of things that were needed in general. Someone to take over the trees along the main street. To hang baskets of flowers in the summer. Lights to trim the trees in the winter months. Sidewalks needed repairing too.

"I had no idea it would get this big." Bancroft asked why she didn't think that. "I don't know. I just figured you'd tell me to sit down and shut the fuck up, or you'd slay me, or something like that."

Kelly laughed. "I made him promise not to slay anyone I like. That would be you." Kelly hugged her. "This is just the thing I was looking for to do. I know it's all your idea, but I want to help you in any way I can. It's so much nicer than digging up the dead and trying to figure out what idiot thought killing them was the best way to settle a dispute."

Lizzy enjoyed talking with Kelly. She was smart and kind. Her way of thinking was so close to hers that she thought they'd get along nicely when things started to roll. While sitting in the living room, waiting on Bancroft to get off the phone, they talked about all the other things brought up at the meeting. When Bancroft returned, he smiled at her.

"There is now a bank account at the local bank that is called simply Repairs. With the donation I made to set the account up, you now have more than fifty thousand in it to start repairs. If you don't mind me asking, could you hire anyone local that knows how to make these repairs? It'll help a lot of families be able to survive the winter coming up." Remy and Lizzy both thought that was a wonderful idea. "Good. The pack of wolves here will benefit from this as well. I like this, Lizzy. Thank you so much for bringing it up."

"You're welcome." He smiled at her, and she could see his fangs. It occurred to her that he looked less like a vampire than any she'd ever seen. Not that she'd met that many, but he looked and acted like a normal person. "Are there many people in town that know what we are? I mean, no one is going to balk at having vampires making these adjustments for them, are they?"

"There are a few, very few, that know. But once this

gets a start, after the first house is fixed, I don't think anyone will care if you're a pixie spreading dust all around to help them out." Lizzy wondered how she could help Hal and his family and decided to look into that. "I can see your mind working. I hope you won't mind Kelly and I working to help you out."

"No. Why would I?" He didn't say anything, but she thought she understood. "You mean because of the way I became one of you? You had nothing to do with me becoming a vampire. And so long as you don't fuck me over, I'll gladly do what I can for the town. I like it here."

"And if I were to fuck you over? What do you think you can do to me?" She snapped her fingers, something else she'd only just figured out she could do. Bancroft was laughing so hard sitting in the cell she'd put him in that she couldn't help but join him. "I don't want to taunt you into having to do better than this, but you know this won't hold me, don't you?"

"How sure are you of that?" She watched him as he struggled with the cell. No matter what he did, he couldn't open the doors or bend the bars. He finally gave up and asked her what she'd done. "I only put it in your head that you couldn't get out. The rest was you."

Lizzy figured she'd only be able to use that once on Bancroft. But it was worth it to have him look at her with a little more respect. Lizzy hadn't felt this good in a very long time, even before she'd been changed. Having someone beside her, Remy made her feel like she could do anything she set out to do.

Chapter 5

Remy kept an eye on Josh as he moved in and out of stores. He'd heard no less than four times that the man was looking for Lizzy. He thought about killing him for all but a second. Remy knew to do that would piss Lizzy off. Talking with the man might be the best thing he could do right now. As he came to the store that Remy was by, Remy asked him if he was Josh Hinkley.

"I am. Who are you?" Remy took his hand into his and felt the man's need for a good meal, as well as his anger at no one helping him find Lizzy. "I've never met you before, have I? I'm usually good with names, but I don't think I know yours."

"Stanley Remy. Most everyone around here calls me Remy." Josh said it was nice to meet him, calling him Remy three times. "I'm to understand you're looking for Elizabeth."

"No. I am looking for someone, but her name is Lizzy. She and I are to be wed." Remy explained to him that he thought Lizzy was short for Elizabeth. "Really? Well, perhaps I should be asking for her by that name. Then maybe someone can tell me where she is. Her attorney told me she was around, but I've not seen hide nor hair of her. Do you know her?"

"I do. I'm not sure why you'd think you might still be set to marry. Wasn't she gone for like a year? A great deal could have happened between then and now." Josh told him they'd had an agreement. "An agreement? That doesn't sound all that loving. Does it to you?"

"We were settling. Mostly me. I could do so much better than her, I think. But when I asked her, thinking she'd turn me down flat, if she'd marry me, she said yes. Now that I've had time to think about it, I think it'll be a good marriage. How do you know her?" Remy asked him if he thought it was going to be a good marriage, why was he looking for her. He thought they should be together already. "You'd think that, wouldn't you? But she's been missing. For a while, I thought she was dead. No one had seen her, nor had they spoken to her. But her attorney assures me she's alive. I need to get a few things cleared up with her, like setting a date for us to wed."

"I see." Josh looked over his shoulder, and Remy looked too. It was Kelly and Lizzy coming toward them. He asked her not to say their names; he was playing with Josh a little.

"Now, there are some beautiful women. Wouldn't you agree?"

"They are. One of them is my wife." Josh told him he was one lucky bastard. "Yes, I think so as well. The other woman is the wife of a very good friend of mine. You might have heard of him. His name is Bancroft Dalton?"

"Yes, I have heard of him." Remy put his arm around Lizzy's waist as she leaned against him. "From what I heard about him, he's a very generous man with his money. You can do that when you have it all, I guess."

"What do you know about my husband?" Josh stuttered when Kelly asked him about Bancroft. "If you'd not mind, I'd rather you kept your opinions to yourself. You don't know him or anyone well enough to form nasty comments like that."

"I meant no harm. I swear it." Josh kept looking at him, then at Lizzy. When he smiled at her, Remy was positive he had no idea he was standing next to the woman he'd been looking for an entire year. "You are beautiful if you don't mind me saying so. I bet you look familiar to me because you're a supermodel or an actress, aren't you? Come on, tell me why I think I know you."

"You do know me, moron. I'm Lizzy Strickland Remy. You've been all over town telling people I'm dead. Well, here I am. What is it you want?" He just stared at her. Remy thought it was funny that the well named moron asked Lizzy if she was sure. "Of course, I know who I am. Apparently, you don't. What is it you want that has you going all over the place telling people you're looking for me?"

"You and I are supposed to be married by now." Lizzy told him she was married to Remy. "No. See, you can't be. You and I, we had a date set up and everything. Then you disappeared and left me holding the bag. I just realized something too. There were gifts I should have had a part of. Are you keeping them away from me as well?"

"There were no gifts, Josh. I never sent out the invitations. For that matter, I didn't even have them printed up. Marrying you would have been a mistake for you and me both. I think one of us wouldn't have survived the first day." He asked her if she meant the wedding night. "That's it. I was telling you that you'd never survive having sex with me. Is that all men think about?"

He and Josh answered her at the same time, both of them saying yes. She smiled at Remy but glared at Josh. The poor man didn't know what to think with Lizzy being so honest with him, he'd bet.

"I was going to live with you in your home. You have so many people living there now that no one will let me in." She told Josh it was because he wasn't going to be welcome there. "But why not? We had a deal."

"The deal is done, Josh. I don't believe you ever asked me to marry you anyway. You sort of ordered me to do it, so you'd not be stuck with finding a date for business functions. Have you been working at a job at all that would require you to go to some function? I don't think you have." He said he was going to work for her. "Doing what? I don't think you're qualified to do anything I need done. There will be jobs coming to town soon. Maybe you can get on at one of them."

"I don't want to work at a job, Lizzy. I wanted to just work for you in a husband sort of way. You know, just say that I'm running something that you own but not really doing much? That would suit me better, don't you think?" She rolled her eyes at him. "Come on. You could use a good man in your corner, couldn't you?"

"I could, and I have one. Remy is going to help me with all the things we both are working on." She asked him why he thought she would keep him with money. "I mean, I did tell you that you'd not be getting into my money when you set this hair-brained idea up."

"I don't understand you. You can't just leave me hanging like this. Do you have a sister or something I can attach myself to? Someone that has money. That will have to be something I have." She asked him why he'd need money. "I told you. I don't want to have to work at a real job. I mean, just looking for you all this time has been exhausting. I know. Maybe you can just give me a pretend job—one like I was talking about. I just show up, and you pay me for doing a job. I'd want benefits as well."

"No." Remy laughed when Josh pouted. "I would suggest you find yourself a job before you find yourself homeless, Josh. I did have you researched. Are you aware that you're currently behind in your rent by six months? Not to mention, while you've been using all your job hunting time looking for me, your power has been turned off. Not that it matters, I guess, since you've been kicked to the curb. You know you're going to have to pay the back rent as well as the power bills, don't you?"

"I was hoping you'd get me caught up." She again told him no. Josh looked at Remy. "She say that to you all the time too? I mean, does she ever agree with you on anything you might suggest to her?"

"All the time." Josh asked him what his secret was. "I keep her sexually satisfied all the time, and I don't need her money. I have a great deal of it all on my own." Kelly laughed and said she'd see them later; she had to get some things from the store. When she walked away, Josh stared at her ass. "I'd keep my eyes off that one if I were you, Josh. Her husband will tear your throat out if he finds out you've been eyeing his wife."

"What? A man can't look anymore?"

Josh looked at Lizzy in the same way. Before Remy could tell him he had better not look at his wife like that, Lizzy picked Josh up with one hand wrapped around his neck. As he struggled, Lizzy spoke to him.

"I believe this world would be better off without this sort of shit around all the time, don't you think?" Remy pointed out that Josh couldn't breathe. "Well, it's not like I'm going to starve his brain of oxygen. His ass is free to get as much as it can while I hold him here. But I guess you're right."

Josh landed on his ass and sat there, gasping for air as he glared at Lizzy. Remy put out his hand to help him up, and Josh stared at it like he was looking for the knife he might stick him with. Remy told him he was only going to help him up. After he was standing on his own two feet, Remy squeezed his hand hard enough to hear bones break.

"Stay the hell away from my family. That would include my wife and my friends. Do you understand me?" Josh nodded and told him he was hurting him. "I am, but you're still alive. Look at me."

When he did, Remy could read his mind. He didn't do it gently either. After getting all the information he could from the man, he let him go. Josh was nursing, not just his hand, but his bloodied nose as well.

"His plan is still in place to marry you. Then he's going to murder you. Well, have someone murder you anyway. After that, he's going to move into your home and sell off everything he doesn't like. I'm not sure how that is going to work, as he hasn't any idea what you have in the house." Lizzy kissed him and then walked away. "Don't you want to know what else he was planning?"

"No. He's no longer a threat to me or you." Remy looked at the man as Lizzy continued. "Let him go, Remy. I'm sure that in no time at all, he's going to have all his terrible deeds catch up with him. Then he'll have to face his own maker. Come on. Let's look around at the buildings Bancroft is donating to the town and figure out a plan."

Remy walked away, something he didn't think he'd have been able to do only a few weeks ago. Josh didn't matter to him. He was nothing. Any actions he tried to take against Remy or his family would end his life, something Remy could live with. As they entered the first building, he realized how good it felt to walk away from conflict.

"Thank you." He asked Lizzy what he'd done to be thanked for. "You kept me from tearing his throat out. Kept me calm too. I didn't realize how much I was forever flying off the handle until I met you. It's a good feeling."

"You did the same for me. I was just thinking about how I was able to keep from killing him myself. Not that I don't think it might yet happen, but for now, I'm not concerned with him." She kissed him again. "You keep doing that, and I'm going to think you want me to take you right where you're standing."

"That would be wonderful, but not practical. I have to get this building thing figured out today so Bancroft can get the paperwork started. His grandma is going to run the food pantry now. She said she won't be tempted to take anything home for her own pantry. That woman is a hoot." He asked her if she'd gotten back already. "Yes. Just this morning. Gwyneth joined me when I was watching the sun come up. She told me she'd enjoy visiting me every morning if I'd allow her. Like I think I could stop her."

"She's been a wonderful grandma to me as well. Gwyneth and Bancroft have been there for me so much I call her Grandma as well." Lizzy told him she'd asked her to do the same. "I thought she would. All right, my dear. What are you thinking of this building?"

They went through all three of them in just under an

hour. Lizzy made notes on what she saw that needed to be repaired in each of them, as well as the things each building had that would be helpful. The second one they looked at had the most features, but it also needed the most repair.

"I'd hate to think we'd do all these repairs and then the entire idea flop." Remy hadn't heard her doubting anything since he'd met her and asked her about it. "I don't know why I'm thinking that, to be honest. It's a scary thought to have usage of that much money and how we're going to be using it. Don't you think?"

"I think that now the ball is rolling, you can count on not only this working but the other two projects going on as well. If it makes you feel any better, I can tell Bancroft we'll pay for the repairs on it. He'll object just so you know, but I can offer." Lizzy said that would make her feel better. "Then I'll talk to him when we get back and show him what we've been able to figure out. Also, you might want to know that Kelly is organizing a few things too. She's been doing some charity work on her own when not working for the Feds."

"She told me. I really like her." He said he did as well. "Good. All right, my dear husband, two things. We should make this marriage official, and figure out what we're going to do with the rest of our life. I love you. Also, I'd like a child or two."

Remy was still standing there when she walked away from him, his mouth hanging open, his heart pounding. She loved him. She said it. And she wanted to have his baby. Remy heard her laughter and decided she was perfect for him. Yes, he thought, he'd been picked to have the most wonderful, perfect wife ever found.

~*~

Bancroft looked over the money from the estate of Richardson. It was up to him to distribute the money now that he was in charge of the league and all that went on surrounding it. There was a great deal more money and other items than he'd been told. That wasn't even counting the homes that Richardson owned, nor the two safes that had yet to be opened.

"I've been able to locate the other women's families. What is left of them anyway." He asked Kelly what she meant. "When the bodies were released from the morgue, two of them weren't picked up. After doing a little research on them, I found out that their husbands had sold their wives to Richardson. If I had my way with them, I'd make sure they were as dead as their wives."

"I'll take care of them." She smiled at him. "Or have you done that already? You are a very sneaky person, have I told you that before?"

"No. But it's good to know I can be one step ahead of you. They're being charged with manslaughter—both of them. Because they profited from the death of their wives, they're as guilty as the man who killed them. There aren't any children, thankfully, so all I had to do was call in a favor." He asked her about the others. "Just after one of them was claimed, her father committed suicide. It's not clear why he did, but it doesn't appear to have anything to do with Richardson. He was all that was left in her family. The other two women are going to be buried within the next few days. Their families could certainly use the money too. These two women have young children, so it might go a long way in helping them get along for the rest of their lives."

"There is a great deal of money here for all of them." She asked him if he had a problem with giving it to the last families. "No, I don't. I just wonder how I'm going to be giving them millions of dollars without some sort of explanation. They don't know a vampire killed them, do they?"

"I'm not sure. I didn't notify them when their bodies were found. Should we research that?" He said he wasn't sure either. "What about a victim's fund? I mean, telling them that since they were killed like they were, there is a fund they can draw on that will help them out. Maybe set up a scholarship in the women's name for them to use for other members of their family?"

"That's a wonderful idea." He made notes on it. "I don't think Lizzy is going to be too thrilled about her cut, either. I might have to have you tell her about it. She's going to get the bulk of the money. Richardson's maker is telling me she should get most of it. Also, because Richardson threatened Remy with the board, he wants him to have restitution for that. I hope never to have to deal with anything like this in the future, love. It's very sad, yet complicated as well."

"Just dealing with the bodies is more than I've had to work with before. Knowing that they were killed by a vampire and not being able to put anything into the records to indicate that had me second-guessing myself at every turn. With Lizzy, however, I bet she turns it into a charity thing too." Kelly came over and sat on his lap. "I really like her, Bancroft. Do you suppose she and Remy will hang out with us some? I mean, I know your friends are coming. Which reminds me, there was a call from someone named Ramon while you were out. Jamison said he'd call you later. Anyway, I'd like to get to know all the people in your life, but having a female friend is something I've not had a great deal of practice with."

"I don't believe she has either. I found out from Remy that the women that were going to be her bridesmaids were people that worked for her. Not friends, not really, just employees." Kelly told him that was sad. "It is. Her life was a good one. She worked hard and made herself something despite not having any family or anyone that even cared for her to fall back on."

"This makes me so happy that I found you. I was so ready to quit a job that I loved, move to a different area, and start over. I know I would not have been anywhere near as happy as I am right now."

Bancroft kissed her and then held her to him so he could assure himself that she was his. There were times in his life when he had wondered if life was worth it. He'd been around for so long that nothing surprised him anymore. Even trying new ventures was boring and nothing to get excited about. Bancroft had gone through life in a series of hops. He'd don one hat, then trade it out for another when that job became mundane. He could admit it to himself now, but he was looking for a job that would, by being the most dangerous he could find, end his life of boredom.

Then he'd met Kelly. To say that she was his world would be grossly understated. She was the reason he opened his eyes in the morning, his reason for facing each day with a smile. The idea of the sort of adventures the two of them could get into or create was exciting to him. Yet, it wasn't only that. It was also the ability to sit close to her. To watch her sleep at night. Hearing her excited laughter, even at his expense. When she pulled away, he stared into her eyes.

"Are you all right?" He nodded, emotionally spent in where his thoughts had taken him. "I love you, Bancroft. So very much." Kelly laid her forehead to his.

"And I love you, Kelly. Every day is a day I think I'll be to the limit of my love for you. Because as surely as I sit here, I swear to you I couldn't love you any more than I do at this moment. But then I see you, and it grows even stronger." She kissed him. "I'm the luckiest man in the world."

After she left him, he sat there for several minutes, getting his thoughts in order. Loving someone, he'd come to discover, was very wonderful. But it was easily a distraction as well. Putting the cash that was all over his desk into the envelopes he'd marked for where it went, Bancroft wondered where he'd start.

"Bancroft? Are you there?" He looked up at Remy and smiled. "I've been here for five minutes, and you were talking to yourself. What are you doing with all this cash? Did you rob a bank?"

"It's the money from Richardson. I was just figuring out how to get it to the families that were harmed by him. Kelly suggested putting a scholarship fund together for the families to use. I think it would go a long way in helping. Did I miss an appointment with you?" Remy told him he was supposed to be taking him to the empty warehouse. "Yes. I forgot. Christ, it's been a very short morning for getting things done. I've found myself several times not even sure what I'd been thinking about."

They were both out the door in less than ten minutes. Talking about nothing much, he was glad his buddy had come here. Bancroft told Remy about getting a call from Ramon, and that he was going to call him this evening.

Entering the warehouse, both of them stopped when the smell hit them.

"That's not a smell I'd associate with being in a warehouse. What do you think it is?"

Bancroft shook his head but looked deeply into the large open room. He could see nothing but shadows. Pulling them around him to enter the room deeper without being caught, he was at the other end when he still hadn't figured out the smell.

"Bancroft, I think it's out back."

He went to his friend and asked him to wait until he went out first. Bancroft told him that if anything were to happen to Remy, he was terrified of Lizzy. They were both laughing when the doors were pulled open. It took Bancroft a few seconds to see what was before him.

"Happy birthday, Bancroft." Kelly tugged on his arm when he just stood there. "I can tell by your face you're surprised. Your grandma told me it was today, and I thought you'd enjoy having a party."

"I don't remember the last time I had a party for my birthday." He kissed her. "I'm assuming everyone was in on it, and that is why you set up me coming here?"

"Of course everyone was in on it. Now come on and mingle." Ramon was there, as well as his friend Donald. All the townspeople were also there, and he was happy to see there was food for everyone. Gifts, he noticed, were for the guests. Each child, it looked like to him, got a toy, and adults were given an envelope. That was the tradition he'd had when he was younger — gifts not for the birthday person, but for those that had been willing to come and spend the day with him in celebration.

The party went on through the night. People would come and go. Everyone seemed to be having a wonderful time. He was glad no one had asked him how old he was. If pressed, he didn't know how close he'd come to the year he was born. His grandma would know, of course, but she'd give him a hard time about it. Today was for celebration, not for having his head popped by his wonderful family.

"I was sure you'd be pissy about this." He asked Lizzy if she would have been. "If I was as old as you seem to be? Yes, I'd be really pissed that someone was pointing out that I was a degenerate."

"I think you mean nonagenarian." Smiling, Lizzy told him she thought she had it right. "Are you ever nice to someone?"

"I thought I was being nice. I mean, I could have called you a pervert. How many years are there between you and Kelly?" She rolled her eyes at him. "Sheesh, Bancroft, talk about robbing the cradle."

Bancroft laughed. Christ, it felt wonderful. He had friends, family, and everything else a man would need, right there where he could see them whenever he wanted. Bancroft vowed not to think of what sort of person he was before, but to focus on who he was now. He knew for a fact that he'd feel so much better if he did. No more feeling sorry for himself, either. Life, even at his age, was too short to squander away.

Chapter 6

Remy watched Lizzy sleep. He knew he had to wake her up, but he dreaded it. The money Bancroft had slipped him last night was between him and his Lizzy. Giving it to her was going to cause some trouble. Not for him, he hoped, but when she hunted down Bancroft. That thought made him smile.

"What's so funny?" He leaned over and kissed her. "That's a wonderful thing to wake up to, but from the look on your face, I'd say you're trying very hard not to tell me something. Why is that? I have never hit you. Tempted at times, really, but I've refrained. Just tell me."

"Richardson's maker decided to turn over the money to Bancroft because he is the kiss leader." She nodded but didn't sit up just yet. "Yes, well, after he divided the money up the way he should have— By the way, did Kelly tell you that two of the wives had been sold to Richardson? That's the most horrid thing I've—"

"Stanley Remy, you're stalling." He grinned. "You're

making me very nervous. Just tell me what sort of damage I am going to have to do to Bancroft for giving me the amount that is going to piss me off."

"You're going to murder him, I think." He handed her the envelope. "I have one as well. Not nearly as much as there is in that one. Cash is the way we usually dish out money like this. It makes it so we can spend it without having to explain how we got it."

"You're babbling again." She opened the top flap of the envelope and then closed it. "There is a lot of money in here. Even if it were all ones, which I'm assuming it's not, that's a great deal of money."

"It's all hundreds and fifties. Yes, it's a great deal of money. As I said, I have one too, as Richardson tried to blame me for making baby vamps and not caring for them." She dumped the envelope on the bed after sitting up. "I like the way it's all bundled up. It makes it easier to know just how much is there. Did you count it?"

"There are two hundred bundles of one hundred dollar bills here, Remy. That's two million dollars. There are—" She counted his hundred bundles. "Remy, there is over three million dollars here. We can't take that. What about the other families?"

"They were all paid too. A million each. Other than the two families where the husbands sold them, and the family of the woman who only had her father left. He killed himself rather than face the world without her." She glared harder. "Plus scholarships have been set up to help the victims and others. That makes it easier to explain to someone that a victim's fund is where the money came from."

"I don't want this." He pulled the other three envelopes out from under his pillow. "If that's more money, I'm not going to be happy. I mean, I love having money, but not at the expense of someone being killed for it."

"It's not cash, no. However, I am to point out to you that you ended a reign of terror that might well have gone on for a lot longer. You killing Richardson saved a great many lives." She told him he was full of shit. "No, listen. He was a vampire, the same as us. He could have, and more than likely would have, kept doing what he was doing for who knows how long. There wasn't much that could have gotten around him. To kill him, I mean. His maker, Robert, said that you saved him face. Also made a name for yourself in the world of vampires. I'm not sure what that means—I forgot to ask—but people will know better than to fuck with me because I have you in my corner."

"Very funny." He didn't tell her he was serious. Letting her think that he was pulling her leg might save him from being hurt too. "What the hell am I supposed to do with this much money, Remy?"

He pushed the other three gifts closer to her. When she opened the first one, he watched her face as she read the letter that had been handwritten by Robert. He'd had one as well. A long thank you for doing a job that he should have figured out a while back.

"Robert says here that he has taken care of the other victims, the ones that had been killed before I helped him. There were thirty more murders on this guy's list." Remy saw a small tear roll down her cheek. "He also says that he's indebted to me, and will be so long as he lives. That having a small kiss, as he does, doesn't excuse him from not paying attention to what was going on inside of it." She looked at him. "What would him being indebted to me mean?"

"Usually, it means that you can count on him to be at your side, with his kiss, should you need an army. Also, if you need a favor. Most people don't bother with asking a vampire for a favor, as you can well understand." She nodded and folded the letter up before putting it back in the envelope. The second one was filled with deeds. "I got one deed to a place out west. It's about seven hundred acres, I guess—more land than I have any idea what to do with at the moment. I used to be a cowhand. I have no idea why I thought that would be a good job. It's hot and smelly. Anyway, I have that."

"These are homes, all of them—homes all over the world." She looked at him with such a sad expression. "I do hope that no one that owned these homes before him was killed so he could own them."

"They weren't. I had a feeling something like that would bother you. It would me as well. But no. He purchased the houses with money and has had them updated every ten years or so. One of them is on the list of historical buildings.

He's owned them that long." She was laying them out, telling him the places they could visit to decide on what to do with them. "What a wonderful idea. This will make a great honeymoon getaway as well."

The third envelope was open, and in it was a key. He had no idea what it was about, but the card that was with it said it would open a safety deposit box at a local bank. Lizzy asked him if he knew what was inside it.

"No. I didn't know there was a key to anything. The keys to the homes we own are in separate envelopes with the addresses on them. Also, a list of taxes that are paid yearly by Robert. I tried to talk him out of it, but he'd not have it." He looked at the handwriting on the card. "I don't know this writing. I'd say it's not Robert's. It doesn't look like his."

"I can check on that for you." Hal sat down on his knee as Remy picked up the deeds. "It would be easy for me to slip in and see what's in the box if you would like. To be honest with you, my lady, I'm getting in trouble at home from the other faeries for not having much to do."

"I'm sorry about that, Hal. I'll have lots for you to do soon. You tell the others that for me." He said he would and thanked Lizzy. "I know what I'm going to do with some of the money. With your help, Hal, I'd like to have a forever garden planted. I've seen them before, and I can't think of anything better to give you than all the flowers you want. You saved me too, you know. Had you not come to me when you did, there is no telling where I'd be now."

"You'd have been all right, my lady. All right, indeed." Lizzy told him that he would be welcome to come with them to the bank. "I'd like that. I can spot trouble with the box if there is something in it. Not that I think there will be. Lord Robert, he's a good man. I've seen him taking care of his people well. I don't know how that bad one slipped by him. He must have been having a bad day."

It had happened over a decade for Richardson. It would have been a bad time for a lot of people all the way around, Remy thought. But he didn't say anything to Hal. Remy liked Robert. He didn't know him well, but he was a nice enough person.

After getting dressed in warmer clothing, the three of them set off for the bank that was on the card. He and Lizzy were trying to think about what might be inside the box. However, after a few minutes, they were starting to be silly. Laughing as he entered the bank, he knew immediately that something was wrong.

"Hal, go tell Bancroft there is a robbery at the bank." Hal flew away just as the two men wearing masks told them to come in and shut up. "This is a bad idea, guys. You know you're not going to live long enough to spend what little you get out of here."

"Oh, and what do you know about this?" Remy sat where he was told, but Lizzy didn't want to sit on the floor. The man he'd spoken to first lifted his gun back as if he was going to hit her.

"I have had a really good morning so far, and you're

not going to fuck it up for me. You even move that gun in my direction, and you'll never see me killing you." The man laughed, turning to his partner to see if he thought it was funny too. "You won't think it's so funny if I remove your head, and you have to stare at your body until it falls to the ground."

"Honey, it doesn't work that way. People think it does, but in my experience with removing heads, both parts are just dead." The man with the gun watched he and Lizzy as they talked about whether or not a person could see his body after losing his head. "Of course, I've never had a firsthand experience at having my head removed, and they're in no shape to answer that age-old question, so it might well happen."

"What the fuck is wrong with you two? Can't you see that we're robbing this place, and we have guns?" Lizzy told him to not be rude and interrupt someone when they were talking. "Excuse me? I'm in charge here."

"Because you have a gun?" The robber looked at the gun as if he was making sure that he really had one, then nodded at Lizzy. "That only makes you armed, not in charge. If you were even remotely in charge, I'd be doing just what you told me to do. Do I look like I'm afraid of not sitting when you told me to? No, I'm not. Now hush while I talk to my husband."

"What's wrong with her?" The man looked at Remy, then back at Lizzy as he continued. "Doesn't she know I'm going to kill her if she doesn't cooperate?"

"I'd say that should you even try to make her cooperate with this travesty you're doing, then you're much dumber than I first thought." He asked him if his wife always wore the pants in their family. "We take turns. It's her turn to knock a bad guy on his ass. Tomorrow is mine. You're just lucky it's her turn today. I would have killed you right off the bat."

"You two are nuts. Has anyone ever told you that before?" Lizzy told him they were the smart ones, as they weren't trying to rob a bank. "I am robbing this bank. I'm going to get into the safe too. The two of you are going to get us out of here by being our shields."

The man thought that was funny too. Turning to the other man, he told him to pick up his gun. When he shook his head, his partner asked him what the hell was wrong with him.

"You might not have noticed it, but us getting out of here in one piece has flown out the window. Look outside, Bret. There are about fifty cops out there, and they don't look none too pleased that we're in here." He told him not to say his name. The man looked at Lizzy as he continued. "I think it's a little late for that to be a secret. My name is Jefferson Aims. That there is my brother, Bret Aims. I'm giving up my gun. I don't want to die. I have a wife and two little babies at home, and even if I go to prison, there's a chance I can see them grow up."

"Smart man." Lizzy turned to Bret. "You have a chance of getting out of here with only prison time too. Put your gun down, and I'll make sure to let the police know you were cooperating with us."

"Do I look like I was born yesterday, lady? If you think that's all it's going to take for me to get out of here now, then you're stupider than my brother is. We're robbing this bank, and then I'm going to murder you." Lizzy just stared at Bret. Remy didn't know what her expression was, but whatever it was, Bret backed away from her. "You're not going to get close enough to hurt me, lady. I'll shoot you before you do."

"Are you sure about that?" She took a step toward Bret, and Remy stood. He pointed to the front door that was currently out of view of Bret and helped the other hostages escape. He heard from Bancroft as soon as the last person exited the building.

You seem to have this under control. How many are in there? Remy told Bancroft what was going on. *Your mate is nuts. Why is she playing with this man if he is so sure he's going to rob the bank?*

I think she's trying to convince him to give himself up. I'm sending out his brother next. Don't let him be killed, Bancroft. He has a wife and two children that he wants to see grow up. He gave up his gun, which I have when he realized this wasn't going to work. Bancroft said he'd still see jail time. *I'm aware of that, and so is he. He will still get to see them, he said, and wouldn't if he was dead. Smart man there.*

Lizzy had backed Bret against the wall, and he wasn't happy about it. Bret was still threatening her, but he no longer held his weapon up like he was going to kill her. Not that he could, but he didn't know that.

"Your brother is safe." Bret looked around and realized there wasn't anyone in the bank but the three of them. "Put the gun down, and we'll walk out of here without a shot being fired."

"They're going to send me back." Lizzy told him that was what happened to idiots. "I'm not an idiot. I'm a man that needs money. I wouldn't be robbing this place at all if I had a job and some way to feed my family. You look rich. I bet you've never gone hungry because you thought feeding your kids was more important than you eating."

"You'd be wrong." He snorted at her. "I tell you what, Bret. You give up your gun and go out peacefully, and I'll personally see that your family is taken care of until you get out. Then I'll hire the two of you to work at one of my businesses."

"Why should I believe you?" Lizzy told him he really had no choice in the matter. "You're saying that even though I threatened to kill you and that husband of yours, you'll give me a job? Lady, I'm a man who has had few choices in this world. If you're fucking with me, I'm going to haunt you for the rest of your life."

"Put the gun down, Bret." He did, laying it on the floor then kicking it toward him. Remy picked the gun up and laid it with the one that Jefferson left behind. Lizzy put out her hand. "We'll shake on the job and that I'll take care of your families. You have my word that I will do just what

I'm telling you I'll do."

Remy hoped the man would take her hand. When he finally did, he burst into tears as he dropped to his knees. Remy had never been without funds. Never been in a situation that would make him choose death to keep his family safe.

When the police came in, they took care to make sure that Bret wasn't harmed. He supposed that had a great deal to do with Lizzy ordering them around. When he was cuffed and read his rights, Lizzy asked him for his address.

"Please. Please help them."

Lizzy promised she would as the man was taken away. Whatever she wanted to do for the family, Remy would be right there with her, making sure the family was more than happy with their new arrangements.

~*~

Shifting through the paperwork concerning the money she'd been given, Lizzy kept coming back to the Aims families. While they'd been at the house Bret's family was living in, she saw things that rammed home the reason the man had gone to great lengths to make sure his family was taken care of. It broke her heart to see that his children were suffering as much as their parents had been.

She had to make sure there wasn't another incident like this one, where a person's only choice was to rob a bank or to do something equally dangerous to make sure there was enough money for food to put on the table. Getting up, she made her way to the kitchen to get a drink, and for the first time since she'd been changed, she reached out to a person. Kelly would help her. She hoped so, at least.

I was just thinking about you. Grandma Dalton is here with me. Want to have an early lunch with us? Lizzy told her she'd love to join the two of them. She also mentioned that she had a project she wanted to talk to her about. *Sure. We've been working all morning on some projects Grandma Dalton has going now. This will fit right in with what we're doing now.*

Driving to the restaurant they'd agreed on, she was happy to have someone to talk to. Not only that, but it was easier to get things finished when they were all willing to help. Lizzy didn't know how the other two women were going to like her idea, but she thought if anyone would tell her it was a bad one, it would be these two.

They pulled up just as Lizzy was getting out of the car. They didn't talk about business at first, which didn't upset her as much as she thought it should have. Lizzy was a person who got down to business and then moved on to something else. However, she knew that rushing these people would get her nowhere, so she sort of went with the flow. It wasn't until dessert was declined that they pulled out notebooks and began working. They let her tell them what she was thinking about.

"For the most part, people that go into prison leave behind a family. Not all, I know, but the ones thinking that robbing a bank is the only way to get food on the table. I think we need to figure out a way to make them productive parts of society, so that isn't a last resort for them. I don't mean every one of them, but a few." Gwyneth asked if she meant the Aims boys. "Yes. I guess they would be the ones I'd like to start with. I visited their families after they were taken to jail, and it was worse than I could have imagined. It's no wonder they thought that was all they could do. Their landlord had raised their rent again, and there was barely enough money for rent and food. Bret is an ex-con, so he couldn't get a job at all. I want to do something so, I guess, these people don't resort to violence when they think all hope is gone."

"The food pantry could help them some." Lizzy explained to Kelly that in order to get the food, they had to have a car. "Oh, I guess I never thought of how they got there. That's a great point. So do you have any ideas to make it easier for them? I'm all in for helping anyone that is willing to help themselves."

"My point exactly. I have an idea that we can put them to work on some projects around town that will generate an income for whoever can work. Getting to and from work would be the first thing we'd have to insure them. That is where we'll need to begin." She told them she was going to see the judge for the Aims boys. "I think I can sponsor them in some way that they can work off their jail time while providing for their family at the same time."

"What kind of projects are you thinking about? I'm betting very few of them will have a skill that will get them a good job." Lizzy said she knew that Jefferson Aims had been a roofer, and his brother had been a house painter.

"You want to start a construction type of job for them to work? I like that idea, but how many people around here are going to be thrilled about having an ex-con in their homes?"

"I think we could start them off with the empty buildings we're going to be using for the larger pantry area. As well as the deconstruction of the two buildings that have been marked for tearing down." They were both nodding like they were thinking it might work when she continued. "We'll have others around the town come in too and show them a job skill. Not something that would be too complicated at first, but something like hanging wallpaper. Laying bricks for a patio. Things that would keep them busy, but not be like a menial job that would bore them too quickly. Also, I'm thinking if we can work this out, we'll have more people want to use them in their homes when they realize how much they can do."

"You've put a lot of thought into this. I'm liking it so far." Lizzy smiled at Gwyneth. "That doesn't mean I'm going to endorse it. I need more details for that to happen. I no more want anyone else hurt than I do you. But I want to be sure that when putting these men into a situation where there will be items lying about to fence, they won't be tempted."

"I understand." As she handed them both a copy of what sort of skills she thought could be taught, she also mentioned that Bret couldn't read. "That would be something that can be taught to him. It must be really frustrating for him to not be able to read a want ad. Not to mention being able to fill out an employment application."

They talked for three hours. Not just on her project, which she was going to get help with, but also two that Kelly had going. The food pantry wasn't resolved yet, but she knew they'd be getting back to it before they left. One thing she was learning from these women was that they didn't like to leave things open. Neither did she.

"I've got an idea about the food pantry. It won't work for perishables at first, things that need to be cold, but what if we turned a bus, like a school bus, into a traveling grocery store? It would have in it the basic needs, as well as a few extras." Gwyneth asked how that would work. "You mean, how would we take it? I don't know that yet, but I can see ripping out all the seats in one and putting in shelves. I don't even think that would be too difficult to have done. Your two guys could more than likely figure that out. But we'd fill it up and take it to the houses that have requested help. Even if there are special needs, such as baby food or diapers, we could have those packed away as well."

"I love that. Not only would they be able to get just what they can use, but they'd be able to get enough for their families. That's perfect, Kelly." As they continued on that project, they realized they'd need two buses—one for people to get into town for doctors' appointments and to go to the pharmacy. "If we could arrange for them to have their appointments lined up on the same day, it wouldn't have to be run daily. We could use it on other days for things like you were saying, kids and infant needs."

By the time they were ready to leave the restaurant, they were ready to start several things. She had an appointment to speak to the judge in the morning, and she hoped he'd see that what she was proposing was something that was going to help not just these two men, but a lot of families in the area.

Remy was waiting for her when she pulled into their driveway. She excitedly told him about everything they'd figured out, and he was just as excited as she was for it. He told her that he even knew how to drive a bus. He didn't think it would cost all that much, as she'd thought, to renovate one in the way they needed.

"You're a brilliant woman. I need to tell you that more often." He pulled her onto his lap and held her. "While I have you here, there are a couple of things I forgot to tell you about myself. First of all, I'm a lord. That would make you a lady. Also, I have a castle."

"What?" Remy smiled at her and repeated what he'd said about them being a lord and lady. "You know that's not what I mean. What do you mean, you have a castle? A real honest to goodness castle?"

"Yes." He frowned at her jokingly. "Is there any other kind of castle? I mean, do you know of a— Ouch, that hurt!"

"I'm going to pinch you harder next time if you don't stop teasing me. Where is this said castle?" He told her it was in the south of France. "Is it something that can be lived in? I mean, is it in good enough shape that we could go there and spend some leisure time? It's not a crumbling mess of a castle, is it?"

Laughing, he told her it was in great shape the last time he saw it, which was only a couple of years ago. He explained to her it was furnished too, but he didn't know the condition of the furniture.

"What made you remember it?" He said he'd been going over his books. "Do you own a lot of places? I mean, I do own a few, more now, thanks to Richardson, but do you have a lot?"

"No more than I told you about already." She kissed him and leaned back on his chest. "How would you like to go there and be a lady of the castle?"

"That would be great, but I'd really like to be able to get things settled around here first." She told him all the things she had to get going on. "If you help me, I'll get done twice as fast."

"No, you won't. You'll just have more time to think of something else that needs to be done. I'm willing to help you with anything you have going on. You know that." He was right, and she loved him for it. "I'm going to arrange for us to be there in the new year. That way, it will be a good visit where we can have a fire in the huge fireplace and have a long rest."

"All right. In the new year, then." She turned and looked at him. "What about the holidays? Do you guys do anything together to celebrate?"

"Nothing I can think of. I'm sure that when we were younger, we did have something with Christmas, but not Thanksgiving. I don't know why, but we just never celebrated that particular day." Lizzy asked him if he'd mind if they invited some of the townspeople to their home for food. "No. That sounds wonderful. Is that what you did before you were changed?"

"I did, yes. When I was in the orphanage, all of us would be invited to homes to be able to celebrate with a family. It didn't work out as well as any of us thought it would. I'm not being ungrateful, but the children, if there were any, hated us being there. The adults would sometimes use us as servants for a party they were holding, pointing out how they had brought the homeless to their house for the day. It was something I avoided until I left there." He told her he was sorry. "Me too. But when I have people over, there is an open buffet, so no one is having to serve anyone. The food is made by my staff, and they enjoy it as well with their families."

"Great. I like that idea." He kissed her again before setting her aside and getting up. "Now I'd like nothing more than to take you to our bedroom and make you scream a few hundred times. You all right with that?"

"I'll race you."

She was nearly up the stairs when he grabbed her from behind. When he flipped her over his shoulder, she was laughing too hard to breathe. As soon as Remy tossed her on the bed, she reached for him. There was never a person she loved more than she did Remy.

Chapter 7

Remy could spend hours touching Lizzy and still find new places on her that he'd missed. Her skin was silky smooth, and there was not a flaw anywhere on her. Even the mark at her throat that deemed her claimed was beautiful. When she laid out for him, naked as she was now, all he could think about was that she was his forever.

"You have the most wonderful hands, Remy. They're not soft and smooth, but rough and strong. When you massage my muscles, it feels like heaven." He moved his hands up her leg to her ass. "Yes, that's wonderful."

Kissing the firm muscle, he massaged her. Moans coming from her made his cock hard, but he wasn't in a hurry like he usually was. There were times he'd be so ready there wasn't much time for foreplay. Not that she ever complained, but he wanted this to be all about her.

Remy worked each muscle before he moved on to the next one. When she seemed as relaxed as he could make her, that was when he'd move on to the next set. She was like putty in his hands by the time he made his way to her feet, a place he knew she liked him to massage.

"I'm not sure why you wear heels, love. They make your legs look sexy as hell, but they're not wonderful on your feet. You're abusing them." If she said anything, he didn't understand it. Instead of asking her again, he kissed her calf and played with her toes. "When you're big with our child, I'm going to pamper your feet and then paint your toenails for you. That would be so sexy to me."

"I want to have your child, Remy. I think us having a baby would be perfect." Rolling her to her back, he kissed his way up her leg to her knee. "I'm going to be limp as an overcooked noodle if you keep this up."

He didn't stop, but made his way up her thigh to her belly and licked her navel. She tasted ripe to him, like a peach that was ready to fall from the tree. Remy didn't stop with just her belly but moved up her body to her breasts.

The peaks of her nipples were his favorite part, the way they stood stiff for him to suckle. He loved to lick them then blow his breath over her. Suckling one of them into his mouth, he slid his hands down her belly to her pussy and slid inside of her.

Her quick climax brought a smile to his face. Lizzy was so responsive that he loved it when she seemed to be caught off guard when he made her release. Her cries fueled him in some way that made him want more. When he kissed his way down to her pussy, she stiffened in anticipation of him tasting her.

She was soaking wet for him. Her pussy gave off a scent that would drive him over the edge of reason. Drinking from her, licking her, Remy thought that he could easily live off her nectar for the rest of his life if he had to. Lizzy was everything and more that he'd ever wanted in a mate.

Every time she came, he would lap her up. Each time he touched her, sliding his fingers deep into her, she'd beg him to stop. He knew she didn't want him to stop but really wanted more. Remy gave her all he could before he was ready to have his own fulfillment.

"Please, take me." He assured her that he was. "I need you. I want everything you have. Please, Remy. Take me."

Filling her was easy as she was so wet and ready for him. Even as he moved in and out of her, slow at first, then quicker, Lizzy held onto to him as he took her. Her eyes, dark with passion, seemed to look into his soul as she moved with him.

Moving his hand to beneath her ass, he pulled her closer. Her legs wrapped tightly around his hips until she was taking him as deeply as he could go. When she bent up, nearly double, she dug her nails deep into his flesh until he felt the trickle of blood slide down his back. Remy offered her his throat.

The bite was what brought him over. Remy joined her in a release that had them both crying out, their bodies so tight together it was difficult to see where he ended, and she began. As she came a second time, he licked her throat. As he did the same to her, biting her deeply, Lizzy came screaming out his name as he came twice more before falling atop her.

He rolled to his back, pulling her with him. As she laid over him, he knew she was awake because she ran her fingers up and down his chest. Remy pulled her up to him so he could seal her wounds as she did the same for him. Neither of them seemed to be in any kind of hurry to either get up or move onto the bed deeper to rest.

"I've been thinking of you all day." He kissed the top of her head as she continued. "This morning, when I got up, I thought of you out somewhere working, and it thrilled me to no end that you trusted me enough to be there when you needed me."

"I love you. And needing you around is something I never thought I'd have. You're perfect." She looked up at him. "You're also the most beautiful creature I've ever seen."

"Are you buttering me up for something?" He laughed when she did. "I went to the bank today. The bank manager was so grateful to us for helping out with the failed robbery that he was nearly falling all over himself, trying to be helpful. The box we were to open the day of the robbery attempt had another key in it." She rolled to her back, and he leaned up on his side to look at her. "Before I was able to get to the stuff we were supposed to be getting, I had to open five boxes before I got to the one that had gems in it. A great deal of them. Not only that but jewelry as well."

"Did you leave it there?" She got up and pulled a large

case out from under the bed. Opening it, Remy could only stare at the contents. "This was in one safety deposit box?"

"No. It was in four. I stopped after the case was full. I don't know how many more there are. Each one I opened had some gems in it, as well as a key with a number on it. I was actually terrified to go on looking." Remy pulled out what looked to him like a necklace of rubies. They were dark with age and strung together with a gold chain. "There is one like that in emeralds as well. I don't know what to do with all this. I mean, I have a feeling some of it might belong to some great family estate."

"I don't want to tell you it doesn't, but I don't remember anyone ever claiming to have had a necklace like this taken from them." He pulled out another piece of jewelry. "This is beautiful. I think it would look amazing around your neck with nothing else on you."

Lizzy rolling her eyes at him made him laugh. But when she reached into the bag and pulled out a ring, he couldn't believe it had been just sitting in a safety deposit box for all this time without anyone claiming it.

"Do you think we should get some of this appraised?" He said he didn't know. "Yeah, me either. I mean, as soon as we put it out there that we have some of this stuff, people are going to come out of the woodwork claiming it was stolen from them. What are you thinking about?"

"Nothing. I mean, other than the beauty of all these items, there isn't another thought in my head." He looked at her and smiled. "I know of a vampire that might be able to help us out with this. He's one of the friends coming here to visit for a while. I'll contact him if I can. He'll be able to tell us if this is stolen or not. And if it belongs to some estate that is still looking for it. His name is Clyde. Bancroft might know how to reach him better than I will. What will you do if it turns out that some of this belongs to someone else?"

"Turn it over to them." He nodded and said that was what he'd do too. "There is something else I found in the box that you should know about. It's a couple of knives. I didn't bring them out for fear of being caught with them. They're beautiful, bejeweled and sharp. I can see some medieval queen having them at her waist as a decoration, as well as something she'd know how to use. I haven't any idea why that thought popped into my head when I saw them, but it was all I could think about."

"Then it more than likely is just where they came from. I don't know that Richardson was old enough to have been around during those times, but we were. Bancroft and I fought beside a lot of kings and queens. I'm not saying it was fun, but it certainly wasn't boring." He thought about his armor. "You know, I have a few pieces of history I'd like to bring here. They're in the castle, but they'd be perfect for a conversation piece for this house."

"I'd love that." He nodded and laid back on the headboard. "Well, what should I do with this? I don't feel good about leaving it here in the house, but I don't want it in the bank either. The other day proved they're not as safe as I would hope they'd be."

"I agree. But we could have a safe put in here. In fact, it might not be such a bad idea anyway. With us both being vampires, it will be good to have a place to store things we'd like to keep from prying eyes." Lizzy told him she had a gun safe in the basement. "That's good. But I'm thinking bigger. Like a place where we can store a great many things we'll collect from now on."

Remy put all the things they'd removed from the case back into it. He thought having it under the bed was probably a good idea. Who would think that a fortune of gems and jewelry would be just lying around like that? He took out the ring he'd fallen in love with and put it in his pocket.

In the morning, they were going to be married. After that, they were going to start on the buses. He didn't know how many they were going to need; the number grew by the hour. But he'd do whatever was needed just to make Lizzy happy. She'd told him earlier that the bus garage was donating a bus to them.

"We have to buy a brand new bus for them to replace it, which I think is stupid being that we could use a new one too. But the band hasn't a bus to carry their equipment back and forth to games. They're renting one of those big trucks to do it now, and it's eating into their profits." He said he had seats at the games, but he'd never gone to any. "I love football. We'll go the next time they're home. I know Gwyneth has donated a truckload of drinks for them to sell at the games. She's a softy for kids, I think."

"She is. When we were young vampires, she'd take the six of us out see a play. It wasn't anything like it is now, but we all enjoyed it. She and her husband were always helping out around town. And she sort of took the six of us under her wing when we needed someone to talk to." Lizzy said she could see her doing that. "I don't think there was a time when she wasn't there for any of us. After her husband died, she started traveling a great deal. Sometimes she'd take some of us with her, other times she'd take just one or two of us. It was always an adventure with her."

"I love her too. Kelly is such a nice person, but she can be really firm when she needs to be." Lizzy told him about the lunch they'd had recently. "She was so nice to the staff there. I think she tipped them all before we left. That's the kind of person I'd like to be someday. I'm too mean for it, however."

"I don't think you're mean." She laughed. "You're wonderful. The things you are starting here are going to help a great many people. It's going to also be something that will live on forever."

Remy still had some things he had to catch up on. Things weren't as difficult to work on when he had a place to call his own. Usually, he would have to find a place to work, and then it would be one interruption after another. But having his own office and a place to call his own seemed to be making his focus better. He owed that to Lizzy. She was his rock and the foundation under it.

~*~

Josh was broke. Not only that, but he'd not eaten for a few days except for a sandwich he was able to snatch from the local food stand. It hadn't been very good, but he had eaten every bite of it. Christ, he had never been this hungry before.

Yesterday he'd managed to see Lizzy twice but had not approached her. She was always with that big man—her husband, Remy, Josh remembered. Sitting on the bench shivering from the cold, he thought about his life so far.

He'd been broke before, lots of times. But this was the first time in his life that he could remember being broke for this long. There was no place for him to live and get warm. He didn't have the money for a meal to fill his belly. And the worse thing was, the woman he was supposed to have married was running around town like she owned it. Lizzy might well, from what he'd heard around town.

The man she'd married had money. Not only did he have money, but Josh had also found out that Lizzy had a great deal of it too. Like millions. Why she'd not shared any with him was still a tick in his craw.

"What the hell does that even mean?" He had also begun talking to himself. Josh blamed that on being lonely. He was too. There wasn't anyone he could just hang out with. No one to call him when he was fucking around. Josh wanted to have friends like the ones he could see Lizzy had.

As if he'd called her, she was across the street talking to

one of the police officers that had run him off this morning. Trying to get himself arrested so he'd be able to have a meal and a place to sleep had failed miserably. Josh was a failure at even trying to fail.

When Lizzy came across the street toward him, he tried to straighten himself up. He was a mess and knew it. As soon as she sat down next to him, he moved away. Josh also knew he smelled.

"That's the first nice thing you've ever done for me, Josh. I'm guessing you don't have a place to stay." He told her he was hungry too. "Yes, I guess you would be. Patrick, the officer that told you to move on this morning, called me. He said you were going to end up freezing to death if you didn't get some help soon. I'm going to make you an offer. If you refuse it, I won't offer it again. All right?"

"You going to marry me?" She told him no, she was already married. "Yeah. That big guy. You should know that he is known around town as a vampire."

"He is. I'm a vampire, as well." He looked at her, and she smiled, showing him her teeth that were sharper than needles. "So you see, there isn't any way you would have been able to hurt me, so you should really get that thought out of your head if you want my help."

"I have to find a job, don't I?" She told him she had one for him if he wanted it. "Will I be required to work?"

"Yes, Josh. That's the way a job works. You work, and then you get paid for it. How did you make it this far in your life without someone having you put away?

The things that come out of your mouth borders on me thinking you're mentally challenged." He nodded and looked across the street again. "Do you want me to find you a place to stay and a job, or are we going to find you in the spring frozen to death? It's up to you. As I said, I'm only going to make this offer to you one time."

"I'll take it. It's not like I have much of a choice, do I?" She told him he did have a choice. "Sure. Me working for you at some lame assed job or fucking freezing in the winter because you went and married someone else instead of me. I still don't know why you did that to me."

"I did that to you because you had a plan to murder me after we were married. Not just that, but I fell in love with someone very special. You and I would never have made it, Josh. I don't like you any more than you do me." There was that, he thought to himself. Josh didn't even wonder how she knew that. Lizzy was a great deal smarter than he'd ever thought. "Now, about this job. It's a good one. You'll be working a line at the factory at—"

"No. I don't want to have to be on my feet all day." She suggested another job, one where he would be taking phone calls. "No. That won't work for me either. If I have to sit around all day, I'm going to get swollen feet and ankles. That's not good for anyone."

When she got up and started away, he asked her what she was doing. Lizzy told him she would say a little prayer for him in hopes that when he did freeze to death, he'd not find himself near a roadway. Asking her why brought up vivid visions of him getting run down by a county truck with a blade on the front of it.

"I don't have all day, Josh. Pick a job or not. I really could care less right now. Which is it going to be?" He asked her which one was the least amount of work. "The sitting job. However, it doesn't pay nearly as much. Before you ask, no, I'm not going to make any exceptions for you in the amount of money you make."

"Christ, this is a nightmare. I'll take the factory job. It's not like you're being nice to me about either of them." She called him ungrateful. "Perhaps to you. But I had lots of plans for the money you have."

"Yes, well, too bad. Now. I have written down the information for both jobs. You will be expected to be on time and work a good job. In the first two weeks, you'll be trained, and then after that, they'll start you out slowly and move you up. You should be fully trained and working alongside of others by the end of three months. Otherwise, they'll let you go." He asked if then he'd go to the other job. "I'm helping you get a job, not keep it. If you fuck up, that's all on you. Keeping a job will be paramount to you getting a place to stay, food, and transportation. I can't believe you're not thinking of this at your age, Josh. You should always be thinking of where your next meal is coming from."

"I am. But no one will give it to me." He sighed heavily. "All right. I'll start on this job if you're going to make me. It would be easier on me if you were to just pay me like you do the other people that work for you, and forget the job."

"This place you're working isn't one of my places. I don't want you working for me at all." He asked her why not. "Because so far, you've shown that you're not going to work well at anything. So why should I try and find you a job working for me?"

He didn't have an answer, but he did have plenty of questions. Like where was he going to be staying? How was he supposed to be getting back and forth to work? And most importantly, when was she going to give him his first check?

"There is no helping you, is there, Josh? You're all right with taking all the time, but when it comes to you making your own way, you'd just as soon not do it in hopes of someone else making sure you have all the basic needs." She shook her head. "Why did I ever think you'd be all right to marry? For that matter, why did I think you'd be willing to get yourself up on your own feet and work for a better way of life? You're impossible."

When she left him, he figured she was going to figure out what he was going to do for a place to live. Leaning back on the seat he'd been sitting on daily for the last several days, he thought about his lot in life. Shaking his head, he wondered how Lizzy had messed it up so incredibly badly for him.

She had no follow through, that's what he came up with. Plans had been made and set up for her. Things were all in line with the two of them marrying. He had even gone to the trouble of getting the insurance policies set up so he'd have money after she died. But she had messed that up by getting taken by some idiot that had probably known how hard Josh had worked to get Lizzy married to him.

Josh did wonder how much trouble her husband was having with Lizzy to get things done. But he supposed that ship had drove off, and he was lucky to be rid of her. But she sure could be slow about getting things to him. He looked at the big clock on the courthouse and thought that Lizzy was taking a long time in arranging things. It was just after noon. He couldn't remember when she'd been there with him. Josh thought it had been at least an hour.

Josh decided right then that he needed a cell phone. That way, he could make sure she was aware that not everyone worked on her time schedule. He'd also have a way of ordering some new clothing, as well as getting hot food delivered. Josh realized he should have told her he'd rather live in a hotel of some sort so he wouldn't have to make his bed every day. Those were things she should think of when helping someone out.

Smiling to himself, he thought he might start a business of keeping people on a time schedule when helping someone out. They had to remember that the people out there they were trying to help had things they couldn't stop doing while waiting for them to get in gear. Then he realized that would be too much work for him. There wouldn't be any time for him to take his walks and such.

Looking at the tower clock again, he realized it had been over an hour since she'd left him. Just as he was trying to figure out what to do about Lizzy, he saw her husband pull up in front of one of the buildings he'd been sleeping in. He got up from his seat and made his way over to him. Josh had to pause in the middle of the street when several larger trucks with equipment on them parked right in front of where Remy, he thought his name was, had parked.

"Watch where you're going." Josh thought that was rude, as the street was made for walking across, not for big trucks to park in the middle of. "We're unloading here, Josh. If you want to talk to me, you're going to have to wait."

"I don't want to talk to you. I want to know where Lizzy is. She's supposed to be finding me a place to stay and getting me a cell phone." She'd not said that, but he thought Remy just stupid enough to not know what his wife had said. "Hello? Are you listening to me?"

After about twenty minutes more of waiting on Remy to get finished with whatever he was doing, Josh went back to his seat. The nerve of some people, not answering a question when it was put to you. He had a mind to tell on him. Who he'd do that to was beyond him, but he was just mad enough to go to the police again.

They'd been no help to him either. You'd think with the taxes he paid, he'd be able to crash on one of the beds for a few nights. Josh knew he paid taxes too. It would usually be about half his check when he had a job. They should be grateful he was giving them something to do in this little town. Nothing ever happened here.

The loud crash had him sliding off the seat and under it. He had no idea what had just gone off, but he was surely not going to be hurt by it. There was all sorts of smoke where Remy had been, and he hoped the man had been crushed to death. It would save him all kinds of work. Lizzy would be free as well.

However, when the dust settled, he realized he wasn't that lucky, and that his home, where he'd been staying the last few nights, had been torn down. There was Lizzy and that husband of hers standing together as if they knew they'd both pissed him off. He made his way to them, once again leaving his chair to confront the two of them on their duties.

"You said you were coming back." Lizzy told him she'd done no such thing. "You did. You were finding me a place to live, as well as transportation. You're slacking on your promises, Lizzy. Have you always been like this? Maybe it's good that I didn't marry you."

"You're very lucky that you didn't marry me, you dick head. I didn't say a word about finding you a place to live. Nor did I mention a cell phone. Where are you getting this from? I certainly didn't break any promises to you, because there were none given." He told her about the job. "Yes, you're to start working in the morning. I wrote it all out for you to follow."

He pulled the note out that she'd given him. "It says here that I have to be at work as six-thirty. What sane person sets up a workday at that ungodly hour? I can perhaps do nine, but ten would be better. Here, fix this." She just stood there. Josh turned to Remy. "How on earth do you keep her on schedule? All she's done today is talk to me. I'm still waiting on some money and the transportation she was to set up for me. Also, don't think I didn't notice that you tore down my temporary home. While I might not be living there for long, it was still a rotten thing to do."

Chapter 8

Every time he thought of the look on Josh's face, he would break down in laughter. The man hadn't a clue what changed the Lizzy he thought he knew to the pissed off woman she became when Josh managed to push all her buttons at one time.

"It wasn't that funny." That, of course, would send him off again. The way Lizzy pouted at him at what she'd done. "You have to admit, he was sorry for bothering me. I've never spoken that way to anyone before. I didn't know I had it in me."

"I did." She looked at him over the blueprints they were going over for the new pantry. "You have this quietness about you, just like the one Kelly has, but with curse words added. Christ, some of them, like douche waffle, I swear to you, I'll never hear that word and not think of you."

"Josh really thought I was letting him down because I wasn't finding him a place to live and giving him money. I always knew he was lazy, but this goes beyond that." She laughed a little when he did. "I guess I did call him quite a few names. But I'm not sure it was all that funny."

"It wasn't *what* you were doing, love. It was what you were saying that cracks me up. Like when you turned around to him. That alone should have had him backing off. Then he snapped you by mentioning you getting him a phone, so he could keep you working on his things." She growled. "Yes, that was another thing that should have warned him. You growling like a large beast was a little frightening to me, honestly."

"Well, not that I think it did any good, but I know I told him this time that he was on his own. I can only go so far in helping someone before they're going to have to pick up and get their ass in gear. What do you think will happen to him?" Remy told her he didn't know, but not to expect too much from him. "No. I can't be worrying about a grown man who is simply too lazy to get himself gathered up and doing things for himself. Christ, I'm glad I averted a death sentence by not marrying him. For all sorts of reasons, but I think in hindsight, I would have killed him before he did me. He would and is driving me crazy."

The shelves had arrived just yesterday morning when they were at the courthouse getting married. The men he'd hired to tear the packing off had done an excellent job. Not only were they ready to be put together, but all the paper had been disposed of in the recycling bins for the city.

All they'd done about getting hitched was sign the paperwork that had to be filed and go on their way.

Neither one of them had that many friends except Kelly and Bancroft. Then there were his other two friends that had shown up in the last couple of days. Besides, they were going to have a big dinner with all the families tonight.

"The bus engine has been looked over and checked out. I guess I didn't think about that when I thought I was getting a good deal on the buses." He told her it was something they'd have done to a new bus too. "I suppose. Getting it stripped of the seats has certainly opened up a great deal of room. I had no idea they were that huge when empty."

That was another thing he had loved working on, the bus. He and Bancroft had not only gotten the bench seats out easily, but they'd even been able to take out most of the windows and board those areas up. The camper air conditioning unit was working perfectly. With it, things would be nice and cool in there.

Right now, five men were working on putting the shelves in for the foodstuff. He looked over the plans again when Lizzy walked away. There was something here that they were missing, and he just couldn't locate it. It wasn't until Clyde came up and pointed it out to him that he realized what he was, or in this case, wasn't, seeing on the blueprints for the building.

"You think only one bathroom is going to be enough in a place this big? I've come to talk to your wife. She gave me the biggest bag of gems I've ever seen without it being in a vault or something." He knew that Clyde had been told where they came from, but he loved the shocked look on his face. Lizzy joined them just as Clyde found himself a place to sit. "They're all stolen."

"Well, damn." Clyde laughed but told her not to give up so quickly. "If they're stolen, I'm going to have to give them back. Not that I want to keep someone from their treasures, but using them to fund some of this we have going on would have been nice."

"When I said they were stolen, they were. However, not by Richardson. The people that paid him with them stole them from someone else, who actually stole them from someone too. They're all legitimately yours, Lizzy." She asked him if any of them could be returned to whoever they'd been stolen from. "I would imagine they're all dead by now. However, I'd not do that anyway. There could be, and more than likely would be, repercussions on such an act, being nice or not. I'm sure people would turn on you for even having them. No, you're better off just using them when you need them and keeping what you want out of it."

Lizzy showed Clyde the ring that Remy had pulled out of the things for her. Remy had already gone to Clyde about the ring. It had been stolen by Richardson's maker, Robert. Clyde couldn't figure out how the man had gotten it, as it never came to him that it was anything but belonging to Robert. He wondered at it but figured it meant little now. Clyde said it was beautiful on her and nothing more. Remy was glad for that.

"The other things you're having me look into—I've found the vampire in your lineage. He's still around, but he's not out much anymore. I didn't speak to him, but I have found him." Lizzy asked Clyde where he was. "In the States. That's all I can tell you until I actually hear from him. That's the way finding someone works. Not for the dead. I can find dead vampires, even those that have turned to dust, immediately. That's how I know that Fergus is still alive. He didn't come back to me as a dead vamp."

"Fergus?" Clyde said he was a descendant of a great warrior vampire in Glasgow. "I had no idea that there were warrior vampires. What is it they do other than fight?"

"It's not ever used anymore, the term. It brings up all sorts of memories of them going out onto a field of the dead and dying and killing what was left. However, that wasn't their main job. They would sneak into their camps at night and murder a great many of them before the fight would even begin. Sometimes, just for fun, they'd only make them weak, so fighting wasn't possible." Lizzy asked if they changed some of them. "Yes. But they'd never know it until they were burning to ash when they came into contact with the sun."

"That is very cruel, isn't it? I mean, it must have worked too, but it just seems unfair to have vampires doing all your dirty work." Clyde only had to glance in Remy's direction before Lizzy understood and turned to him. "You were a vampire warrior?"

"Yes. For many years. So was Bancroft. However, he

didn't stick with it as long as I did. It was harder for us to get enough to feed on when most of the cities were on high alert. It was an easy way to keep myself alive." She didn't comment more, so he thought it was a good time to change the subject. "There are more things we have to look at if that's what Lizzy wants. If those things were stolen, I'm assuming the rest of it was as well."

"Yes. I'm all for that." Lizzy smiled at him before addressing Clyde again. "I'm to understand you know how to fence this stuff, so no one knows who it belongs to. I don't want you to get into trouble, but we're using these things for several projects. I wouldn't even know where to begin."

"I have a better idea. You can have an auction. One of the bigger houses would take this stuff off your hands in a heartbeat." She asked him about receipts. "That's going to be easier than you think. I'll get in touch with Robert. He's been around enough to know how to fake a receipt. Because you went to the bank to collect it, you can say that is where you were instructed to find it. A fake will won't be hard to do either. So, as your attorney, I'll say you recently had someone pass in your family, after a long search to find them, and he left this all to you."

"That sounds incredibly too easy." Remy told her the simplest ideas usually had the best results. "Okay, we'll do that then. I don't know what to expect in the way of money from the sale, so I've decided not to count on it very much."

Remy had a feeling she was going to have more money than they could spend. But that was all right too. Whatever they got, it was certainly going for a very good cause. He glanced down at the blueprint and decided they needed large walk-in freezers put in. He figured if they didn't use them at the beginning, that was going to be all right. However, putting them in later would be not just costly, but also hard to do because the walls would be up. Handing it off to Lizzy, he told her what he thought.

This building and the one that had been torn down had been donated to the city by Bancroft. They could well have purchased them, but this way, the city would be able to own it and help out with the pantry's other expenses, such as electricity and water.

Lizzy went to find the foreman to tell him what they'd decided. As soon as she left, Remy asked Clyde what he'd not shared with her. He only had to grin for him to know there had been something.

"There are a few pieces in the lot that have something attached to them that she's not going to like." Remy asked him what that might be. "There is a diamond and ruby necklace that was worn by a woman who was murdered on her wedding night. Nothing that didn't happen a lot. To be honest with you, I just wanted to see her with it on. I think with her coloring and the color of her hair, she could pull it off."

"Are you hitting on my wife?" Clyde said he wished that were true, but he was only stating a fact. "She is stunning, isn't she? We're talking about children too. What else?"

"The vampire in her lineage is alive, as I said. His name is Fergus. However, he's not just in her lineage; he's her father. Ferguson Patrick Strickland used to be called Paddy."

It took Remy a moment to figure out what Clyde was telling him. "You mean Paddy Ferguson, the black beard pirate, is her father? I thought for sure he was dead."

"I think a great many people thought that. However, not only is he alive, but he's a very quiet man that now owns a ranch out west where he raises animals that can be bought by shifters." Remy thought of the man he knew about compared to the picture of the one Clyde was talking about. "Another thing you might want to know is that he hasn't any idea that Lizzy has been born. When word got around to her mother that Fergus was dead, she took the baby to a place to leave her, then joined him in death. Or so she thought."

"Her father? I certainly didn't see that coming. How did he not know she had given him a child? I mean, I thought it was something he'd have been able to feel." Clyde said he had no idea, but he had thought the same thing. "Where was he when this was all going on? I mean, to have a mate carrying your child would be something that would put anyone over the edge."

"That would be something you'll need to ask him, I think. A lot of the things about this are a little off. He's older, too, like your grandma's age. When I found that out, I thought that could have been it. He might have thought he had waited so long there wasn't anyone out there for him, much less him having a child with her." Remy watched Lizzy as she walked with the foreman to show him what she wanted. "Remy, she's going to have to know. I've already put out that I'm searching for him. If he comes here, I'm thinking—because honestly, I don't know with this—but he might well know who she is immediately."

"I'll talk to her tonight. It's doubtful she's going to be really excited about it. But then, I have no idea anymore." He looked at his friend. "Last night, when we were finished talking to Josh, she told me she was finished with him. I thought she'd go find him again and perhaps slip him some cash. Nope. She said she was finished, and she was. He's on his own from now on."

"He's that fool that keeps sitting on the bus bench?" He said one and the same. "Is he planning a trip, or is he really just that lazy that he won't go across the street to get himself a job?"

"That lazy and more so. She even offered him a job. He told her she'd have to provide him with a car if she expected him to work it." Remy laughed. "I have a feeling he's going to end up just as she told him. A frozen human popsicle that a snowplow hits."

Clyde told him he was going to find him some digs. Meaning, he hoped, that he was going to stick around for a while. He hoped they all did. It was nice having someone around to talk to. He did have Lizzy, but he knew having the men around that had shared a bond of friendship for as long as they had would be nice too.

~*~

Lizzy hadn't had this much free time in a while, and she was enjoying it. Of course, she was working. What self-employed person didn't work every second? She was going to be able to catch up on some things, as well as perhaps get a little ahead on a couple of others.

Just as she was putting away one of the many files she'd been working through, the front doorbell rang. She knew it was being answered, but didn't pay any attention. Remy was out with the other guys tonight to find out what they'd all been doing for the last hundred or so years. It boggled her mind each and every time she thought about how old Remy and the others might be.

"Mistress, there is a person here to see you." She nodded. "You need to invite him in. I cannot, as the house isn't mine." Justin, their butler, smiled at her. "I would like to tell you he's harmless, but I know better. However, he will die for you."

That was certainly a strange way to put it, but she got up and went to the front door. The man standing there wasn't anyone she'd ever met before. All she could think about was that he was a vampire, and he was ancient. Like very ancient.

"May I help you?" He smiled at her, not even bothering to hide his fangs. "I don't know you, nor do I care to if you're not going to be at least a little polite. I was extremely busy. State your business and be gone with you."

"I'm here to find Stanley Remy. I was given this address to come to. You'll need to invite me in." She crossed her arms over her breasts and stared at him. "Listen, little girl. I don't have time for your little show of temper. Just— Who are you?"

"Sorry, it doesn't work that way with me. Who are you?" He told her. "Yes, well, Mr. Ferguson, I still don't know you. Also, you might find this hard to believe, but whatever reaction you thought I might have by hearing your name, I don't care. If you want Remy, you'll have to figure out where he is on your own." She started to close the door.

"You look like your mother." Lizzy asked him what he'd said. "Your mother. She even had a little bit of a temper too. Not that she ever used it on me, but she could make a man cry when she was upset."

"I don't believe for a minute that whoever you think my mother was never used her temper on you. You're a rude man. How did you know her? I mean, so far as I was told, both my parents are dead." He said only her mother was. "Then tell me, how do you know her?"

"I'm your father. I might not have believed it except for the color of your eyes. They're the exact color of hers. Are you all right?" Lizzy called for Justin. He came to her so quickly that his movement made her slightly ill. Or at least more ill. "Invite me in, Elizabeth, please? I need to know that you're all right."

Justin closed the door after telling Mr. Ferguson where Remy was. Lizzy asked Justin how he knew who the stranger was. He told her his scent was the same as hers—faded, but the same.

"Did you know he was coming here?" He said only that he knew he'd been found. "I'm assuming Remy knew. As well as...let me see. Clyde. He was searching for him, so he actually found him too. That man, is he still at the door?"

"Yes." She stood up. "I'm sorry, mistress. I thought you'd been told he might show up. Are you going to let him in?"

"I wasn't told shit. Justin, call my husband on the cell he has and tell him that a great vampire is at his home and that I've invited him in. Then hang up. I want him to think about what he's done to me. Oh, and then call Clyde. Do the same thing." He nodded and moved toward the kitchen area. She opened the door. "Would you like to come in this one time, Mr. Ferguson? There will be no biting anyone that lives here, or your invite will be your last to any home."

"Yes. Thank you." She could see the smile tugging at his mouth, but chose to ignore it. Whatever was going on, she was positive there was going to be a lot of head rolling when the others showed up. "Are you always this violent?"

"You have no idea. Have a seat. I don't believe you'll

have time for refreshments even if you were to say that you would like them. You're not going to be here that long." He just grinned at her. "Right now, you might want to wipe that shit off your face. I'm not in a mood to be charmed right now. I'd just as soon pick up the poker by the fireplace and ram it through your head."

"You are quite violent, aren't you? If it makes you feel any better, I didn't know about you. Not even that your mother had conceived." She told him it didn't make her feel better. "I thought not. Would you like to know a little about me?"

"No. Not just yet. I have questions. You will answer them truthfully and not half-truths either. I want answers, not a digging expedition on figuring out the heart of the matter." He laughed again, and she found herself charmed even though she had told him she didn't want to be. "Where have you been?"

"Out west. I have a large ranch out there where I raise mostly cattle, but also horses and other animals that can be used on a shifter's farm. They have to be around them all the time after they're born, or they won't be good for them. Where have you been?" She told him where she'd grown up. "I didn't know. I'm very sorry."

"I've not been a vampire for long, but I have a feeling I should have been. Was my mother human?" He said she was. "Why didn't you stick around if she was your mate? I thought that was a terrible thing to happen to a vampire, to lose their mates."

"I might have guessed she was my mate had I been around when she became with child. But I was pulled, quite literally, from her arms to be sentenced by the council of pirates. I was to serve a term of no less than fifty years. However, about two years after my sentence started, I was set free. I still, to this day, do not know why, but I was out. By then, your mother had died, and I had no knowledge of you being out there." Lizzy asked him if she'd been a turned vampire. "No. She was stronger for being with one, but no, she wasn't a vampire."

Lizzy got up to pace. Remy did it too when he was working through a problem. She figured this was one of the biggest ones she'd ever had. Looking at the man who claimed to be her father, she didn't know what she had to do now.

"Why did you come here?" He told her that Clyde had contacted him and told him to look for a man by the name of Remy. "He's my mate. Husband too. What were your plans for him? Wait. You said pirate. You were a pirate too?"

"Oh, yes. For a great many years. My crew was the wealthiest in the world before I decided I'd had enough of sea life." She glared at him. "Now, what have I done?"

"You had a crew, and you fed from them, I'm assuming. Did they know, or did you dispose of their bodies once you had your fill?" He threw back his head in hearty laughter. He didn't stop either but kept laughing like he didn't want to ever stop. "What the hell do you find so funny now?"

"You are a charmer yourself, aren't you? Do you forever keep this Remy person on his toes? I bet he loves you to pieces, too. Nay, I did not toss them overboard, as you so quaintly put it, but would drink from them when I needed. I was very old even back then, so I didn't need as much as a new vampire does." He laughed again. "They knew who their master was, and didn't care. I think they figured if we were ever caught, I'd just make sure we were freed quickly. Remy didn't kill you when he changed you, did he? That's the way it would have—"

"Remy didn't change me. I was kidnapped and bitten, as well as raped, over a period of time by a vampire who left us all to die. I was the only one that was able to survive. I think I know why now. I had enough of you in me to keep me safe." He stiffened with anger. It was almost so thick in the room that she could reach out and touch it. Even his eyes, a beautiful shade of brown before, were a dark color. Red, she thought. "He's dead now. I killed him when he finally returned to check in on us."

"You killed a vampire? My goodness, you are your mother's child. She did the same before I met her. The monster was trying to get her to allow him to take her to a vampire party. She found out that she was on the menu and killed him for it." She asked him if he'd had such parties. "I don't think that is something we should discuss, Elizabeth. We, as vampires, did many things before we started to get along with humans."

"How did you know my name if you didn't know I

was born?" He said she knew her name. "I do. If you get into my head again without my permission, I'm going to kill a second vampire in my lifetime."

Ferguson was still laughing when Remy and the others appeared in the room. She didn't speak to any of them, but Ferguson introduced himself to them. The only one he knew, it appeared, was Bancroft, but only through his grandmother.

"I'm so sorry." She looked at Clyde and let her anger at him show through. "We were going to tell you. I swear it. But I asked him to contact me first so I could talk to Remy about the visit. I had no idea he'd just show up."

"But you knew what he was to me." Clyde dropped his head and told her he was sorry again. "What if I had run him through because I didn't know him? Huh? Did you think of that?"

"You can't hurt him because he's your father." Lizzy glared harder. "That was the wrong thing to say, wasn't it? I'm truly sorry, Lizzy. I swear to you, when Remy and I talked about it, we were going to see if he got back with us. If he didn't, there was no reason to let you know he was abandoning you a second time."

"But that would have been my decision to make, don't you think?" Clyde kissed the back of her hand, and she felt a connection she'd never had before. "What did you do to me? You know, I'm sick to death of people zapping me with all kinds of shit I didn't ask for. You'll take it back, or so help me, I'll put it back, and you'll never try this trick again."

"I did it, not the young man there." Lizzy stood up and asked Fergus what he'd done to her. "Nothing much. Not really. I laid claim to you. I thought to be able to do it while you were distracted, but you're much more of a vampire than I thought. Have you considered being a kiss leader?"

The growl had all the men backing from her, including her father. When Remy came toward her, she could see that he was just as upset as she was. At whom, she didn't know, but she was still pissed off at the lot of them.

"The next time someone thinks to not tell me something important, even if you think it's not, I will hunt the lot of your dens down and destroy them. I'm not shitting you right now. I'm so fucking pissed off that you're just lucky we have a guest, or this room would be a hell of a crime scene." No one laughed, nor did they think she was kidding. Looking around at the men she'd come to love, she told them to sit down. She decided she needed some fresh air and left the room.

"They're sorry. Some of them didn't even have anything to do with upsetting you, but they're sorry." Remy put his hands around her waist from behind. "I had full intentions of talking to you about him tonight. I swear it. It was also my plan to tell you what we all know about him. Which isn't all that much."

"He was a pirate." Remy said he'd heard that. "Why did you not tell me sooner, Remy? Did you think I'd be too stupid to understand?"

He turned her around quickly and looked at her. "Good heavens, no. I was trying to save you. You've been rejected before when your mother left you behind. I just didn't want you to feel that way a second time if he decided not to come to talk with you. If you want to know, I think you scared him too." She looked up at him and smiled. "Yes, well, he's a very old vampire and has powers that none of us have ever seen. He might well have taken you away from me."

"I would have come back to you. After I murdered him." He kissed her on the nose. "I'm all right now. Did the rest of them leave? I feel foolish for being so pissed off at all of you."

"They're waiting for you to come back. Kelly is here, as well as Gwyneth. She knew Fergus when he was younger, I guess. He's older than her." She asked if he was serious. "Yes. I don't think I want to find out just how much older he is."

"Me either."

They went back into the living room, and she sat down. They were talking now, about the times when they were younger vampires and how they'd managed to survive. Lizzy was glad she'd been turned in this century. She would never have survived the one they were born in. She would have killed everyone given the chance.

Lizzy must have dozed off at some point. She hadn't been sleeping all that well, and usually, sometime during the day, she'd go and take a nap. But this was more than that, she thought. Exhaustion had never been a part of her workday like it was now. She'd have to talk to someone about it before she literally fell asleep standing up. Perhaps all the stress was catching up to her from the last year.

Remy had told her that she wasn't in heat, or whatever they called a woman ready to get pregnant, so she knew it wasn't that. Exhaustion, she knew, was something you didn't mess with. She had been tired for a long time, and it was just now catching up with her. Deciding to rest when she needed it, Lizzy thought she'd be over this in no time.

Chapter 9

Fergus didn't have pictures of her mother that he could share with his daughter, but he did have plenty of wealth. Even though she'd told him she didn't need him to give her anything, he donated a great deal to the charities she and her new husband were working on. Good charities, too, ones that could be counted on to keep the poor healthy and happy.

"You really do like to poke the bear, don't you, Fergus? How are you, old man?" He hugged Gwyneth and asked the same of her. "I'm getting around. Having young people like my granddaughters around gives me a little extra boost. They make me wish I had taken better care that I understood the times better. Do you? Use all those apps on your phone to do things?"

He laughed. "Not as much as I think my employees wish I did. We run a large spread, and sometimes it's just easier for me to go to them rather than try and figure out how to call one of them. The horses are used to me popping in and out, but it still scares the riders." Gwyneth asked him what made him go into ranching. "Nothing much, really. I was with a buddy that was looking for a pony for his daughter, and there weren't any around that he could get because of him being a wolf. I hit on the idea, and it's worked out well for me. As well as little girls that want a pony for their birthday."

"What a lovely thought. I'm assuming you do a good business. When Bancroft was small, he wanted to have a pony. And just as you said, it's not possible for vampires and other non-humans to have such a joy as a pony or any creature like that." He said they also raised cows, pigs, goats, and all sorts of other animals. "I once knew a man that raised trout. I thought him insane for the venture. Then I found out he was selling them to not just fishing ponds or whatever but to restaurants. I should have invested with him when he asked. I just never thought it would take on. I remember a time when if you wanted a fish for dinner, you went and caught one."

They were both laughing, and Fergus was glad for it. "Well, I'm glad he made a success at it, despite you not thinking it was necessary. I have to admit, I might well have turned him down as well. It took me a long time to believe anything was going to change from what I started out seeing."

"Yes. I remember the day it hit me that things were going to be changing, no matter if I kept up with them or not. It was the first time I saw a television. I know what you're thinking, and I did the same. How did it take me so long to figure this out? Well, seeing that thing in my friend's home nearly made me weep for all the things I'd been missing out on." He asked her what sort of things. "There is the icebox. Not that I needed the thing to keep my food cold—I didn't eat enough to warrant it. It was the idea of needing one that I should have thought of. I think that is where I messed up. I saw all these changes coming along, and I couldn't see how it would help me, so I just ignored the progression of things."

"I understand completely. That was my problem too. Not getting out to see the larger picture of the way things could not just help humans, but myself as well." Fergus looked at Gwyneth as he asked her something that had been on his mind for the last few hours. "I've gone ahead and made donations to each of their causes. I was just thinking before you arrived that I don't have anything else to give her, so that would be good."

"You don't have— What do you mean, you don't have anything to give her? I should pop you upside the head. I would, too, if I wasn't afraid of giving you more brain damage. Because there isn't any way, you just said that to me. My goodness, what a thing to say. You have plenty enough to give her, and it's not the amount of the check you've written. I could just scream at you for— What about love? Friendship? Or, for that matter, finding out what she *needs* you to do to help her?"

"Like what? Whenever I ask either of them what they

need me to do, I get this 'We've got it under control.'"
Gwyneth just glared at him. "What did I say now?"

"They do not have it under control. I know for a fact
that something Remy was working on just yesterday is
giving him fits. They're trying to purchase the land next to
the high school, and the board is trying their best to keep
them from it. Something about future projects. Well, I'll
tell you right now, this will be the future projects for those
children." He just loved watching a woman get fired up.
But wisely, he kept his mouth shut and only asked her
what she wanted to do. "Several years ago, there was a
place where the children could go and explore. I'm not
sure when it started to not be used. Anyway, that was for
the younger groups. But for the high school, Remy and
Lizzy thought older children could learn a great deal
about the woods and how they might be able to survive
there. She told us that once she escaped from that man, she
had to figure out all kinds of things in order to live. What
she could use to know the time of the day and such. Also,
what they might be able to eat and drink."

"What a magnificent idea." He did like the idea. Fergus
thought that even a few vampires could use an idea like
this. Not so much the food, but how to find their way when
they were lost. It didn't happen as often as it did when
there were fewer people in the world or cell phones, but it
did sometimes happen. "I should like to help with that."

"Buy the land. Donate it to them and make a donation
to the school for their generosity. Even if you think you've

paid too much, thank them with more money." He nodded, thinking he'd not have a clue how much was too much. "Would you like me to go with you? I'm on the board, though I don't know why. They never do anything but bitch about not having enough funds for whatever project is coming up. You want to know why? Because they only want to do things that are lame."

"What sort of things would you try to make money for the school? Just so you know, you're not alone in that. I believe all schools are not just underfunded, but they are also having trouble finding teachers." She looked at him. "You would be a fantastic person for something like a reality teacher. I don't know that they have those, but it certainly is something I think you'd be good at. I remember my trouble in even trying to balance a checking account. For that matter, I have two employees right now that haven't the foggiest idea of how to write a check. Not that I'm a whiz at it, but something like that would be so helpful."

"I had the same issues. It took me a month before I felt good enough to write one without having to call on Banny to make sure it looked right. And don't get me started on having a last name. I know that's not much of an issue these days, but it was an issue too." They spoke back and forth about things they'd run into while trying to fit in. "I've never really fit in with the women things. I can if I am needed, but I'd much rather just do things on my own. But this teacher idea. I like that. If the school wouldn't allow it,

I could just rent out a building and do it on my own."

They were still talking about her teaching a reality class as she drove them over to the high school. That was something else he'd never learned how to do, drive. There hadn't been much use for them when he could just go where he wanted at any time. A car, a recent addition to the world, was a nasty smelling thing that he just didn't want to fool with.

The teachers were all in their classrooms when they arrived. Just looking in the windows, he wondered how they were able to be stuck in a room all day when there were such wonderful things to discover out of doors. Gwyneth told him that was just what she had been talking about. A way to have a nice class or two out of doors.

Only one of the board members was there, in addition to Gwyneth. She told Fergus she'd wait in the hall while he went in to talk to Malcomb Harley. When Fergus told Malcomb what he wanted to do, the man told him he didn't have time to speak to him about such matters, especially ones that had already been turned down this week.

"Well, I'm here to make you an offer that I don't think the school board should turn down." Fergus reached out to his son-in-law and asked him if he'd come to the school with him. Gwyneth told him that would be a good gesture for the two of them to get closer. "My daughter and her husband were in here, and they were turned down. As a person who is thinking of becoming a member of this town, I'd like to know how a school that is forever low on funding can turn away that sort of money?"

"Look, I'll tell you what I told him. There are plans in the works for that area. Plans that I'm not able to discuss with you." That didn't stop Fergus from figuring out what the plans were by looking into his thoughts. "We, as a school board, are going to hold onto the land so that in the future, we'll be able to use it for what we purchased it for."

"Are you talking about the future plans for the strip mall that is in the works? Or are you talking about the lot the city is planning on buying to put their extra trucks on during the winter months? That's why you won't sell it. You are thinking of purchasing it for yourself, so you can sell it to the highest bidder later." Fergus shook his head. "Neither of those are going to work, you know. First of all, the strip mall won't come to fruition because they'll be using all their funds in just paying for the land. In the meantime, the land will be taken over by people selling their used cars and velvet paintings. Unsavory types will set up businesses there, the kind that are here and gone before the police can catch up with them. Is that the sort of people you want next to a high school where kids can get into trouble? Or worse yet, killed?" He asked him how he'd known that. "Everyone knows what you're up to. If not for you holding things up, the land would be bringing in money as well as being used for something for the students. I don't think a person such as yourself needs to be on the board. There shouldn't be a profit made for helping the children out."

"What do you know?" Fergus told him he obviously knew more than he did. "No. I don't think so. I'm going to be able to finally make some real money from working here. It'll be my little nest egg when one of these things go ahead. I don't know how you got your information, but I'm not taking on any partners, nor am I going to be blackmailed into making sure they get a cut of what I'm doing. This is my idea, and I'm going to run with it."

Gwyneth came into the room without opening the door. Fergus was certain she'd heard every word that had been said. By the look on her face, she wasn't any happier about it than he was. The man was about to get his comeuppance, and Fergus stood back and watched it unfold.

While Gwyneth was busy putting Malcomb in his place, both Lizzy and Remy joined them. Lizzy went to stand with Gwyneth while Remy stayed back with him. He gave him a brief rundown of what was going on, and also why he was there.

"That's very generous of you, Fergus. We've been trying to deal with this man for the last few days. First, he doesn't come to the meeting, then he gets called away. This morning was the first time we'd been able to talk to him, and he just flat out ordered us out of his office." He told Remy how they'd just shown up. Sort of caught him off guard. "It seems to have worked. I didn't know he had all that going on. I should have checked, but I thought it was the school board that was putting us off and not a man that has his head up his ass."

When it was all finished, Malcomb was taken to jail. The only thing they could hold him on was threatening Lizzy. It was enough, however, to get him off the board and someone else in his place. Fergus was very proud that Lizzy took the job offered to her by the other two members.

Cloris Keller had come to the school when she heard on her police scanner that there was trouble. "I would like to propose that we sell this land to Mr. Strickland. He is willing to make a large donation to the school to be used for improvements to the classrooms." Ms. Keller had decided she'd make the motion so there wouldn't be any trouble down the road. "He is offering us a good amount of money for the land, and I see no reason whatsoever that we don't cash in while the money is being offered."

The vote between them was three to zero in favor. Fergus did wonder for a minute or two if they had to have a larger group to vote on it, but as it went in his favor, he didn't care. He turned the project over to Remy, and then wrote out a check for the donation for their generosity. Things were looking up for the school, he thought.

He was just getting ready to go back to the house with Gwyneth when Lizzy walked up to him. He didn't know her well enough to judge her moods or facial giveaways, so he waited while she looked at him. It startled him every time he looked at her as to how much she looked like her mom.

"You didn't have to do this." He was lost in memories

and asked her what she meant. "Buying the land and the donation to the school. If you did it to get me to like you or something then—"

"I didn't. I had hoped you'd like me anyway." She smiled at him. "That right there, Elizabeth, is worth every penny I spent today. But as to what you were saying. No, I didn't do this to win favor with you. I did this because I believe children should be given as much information as they can, regardless of whether or not they're human. I'm sorry you had to learn these things the hard way, but you survived, and that is about all a man could hope for."

Going back to the house later on, he felt like his step was a little lighter, his heart just a little fuller. His daughter was lovely, and she had a good head on her shoulders— two things a man could wish for his children.

~*~

The courtroom was packed. Lizzy had thought there were just too many for the attempted bank robbery and was told it was an all day affair of setting up court dates and assigning fines to people who had only gotten a ticket. She was waiting in the back of the room with both the Mrs. Aims, wives to the two men she was hoping to get taken care of.

It was sad, really, that most of the people were there to either fight a ticket or to get the things settled up for prison time. She'd only just found out that Bret Aims was on his third stint if he were found guilty. Jefferson, his brother, had never even had a parking ticket but had gone along with his brother to get a cut of the money. The guns they had weren't even loaded, not that it mattered now.

The man that stood up when his name was called stumbled his way up to the microphone. He was an elderly man, and he looked to be having trouble seeing. When the officer who arrested him told the judge why he'd been arrested, the judge asked the man if he always broke the law.

"I never have before that day, Your Honor. My wife, she's ill, and I just wanted to see her again. It had been a couple of weeks, and nobody was coming around." The officer explained how Mr. Rogers was to have help daily, but they weren't showing up. Part of the deal was for them to take him to see his wife in the nursing home twice a week. "I called and called to see why they just stopped coming, but got nothing from them. And my wife, you see, she missed me something terrible, and I wanted to ease her heart a little."

The judge turned to the officer. "What were you able to find out from the place caring for Mr. Rogers? I know you, Davy. You looked into it." He grinned and told the judge what he'd been able to understand. "Mr. Rogers, did they tell you they weren't coming? Did anyone come over and tell you that you needed to get other help, as they'd gone out of the business of helping people?"

"No, sir. I got me a house phone and one of them answering machines. Nary a time did I get any messages from them. I just wanted to see my wife." It broke Lizzy's heart the way he kept telling them that. "I ain't got nobody to take me to the store either. If them police officers hadn't come along when they did, I was gonna be reduced to eating my grass clippings out back."

Davy explained that he was indeed without even the basics and had no way to go and get them. He and his fellow officers had not only supplied him with food, but their wives were coming by to make sure he had at least a hot meal daily, as well as going to the nursing home to see his wife.

"Mr. Rogers, do you have enough help now? I mean, you're not going to be driving over to the nursing home anymore, are you?" Mr. Rogers told him he was happy as a camper, as he was seeing his wife more than ever now. And he had himself company at night. "That's wonderful news, sir. Wonderful. If you can promise me that you'll only depend on those pretty ladies to get you what you need, I'm going to dismiss this charge of driving without a license."

"Yes, sir, I promise." Mr. Rogers started crying. He leaned his head on the microphone and sobbed like his heart was too full to contain. "I thank you, sir, for this. I didn't know how I was to see Milly if you put me in prison. I was surely worried about that."

Still crying, he found his seat, thanking the two women that were with him today. Apparently, they were the wives of some of the police officers and had come to support their new friend. Lizzy made a note to see how many other people were breaking the law in order to see their loved ones.

When it was the Aims boys' turn, she stood up from her seat as well. The judge, the honorable Winston, asked her if she was Mrs. Remy, and if she'd been the one that had called his office.

"I am, sir. I'd very much like to speak to you about Bret and Jefferson." He asked her to wait one moment while he refreshed himself with their file. After a few minutes, he looked at her and smiled. "These men, they have been dealt a dirty hand, and only wanted what was best for their families. Since that day, I've been able to find out that Bret has lost his job because a woman he worked with said he'd made an advance toward her. Turns out, she was lying to get him fired because he'd been hired over her boyfriend. Jefferson has two small children, Your Honor, and one on the way. They have no insurance, nor do they have any transportation if they were to find jobs."

"According to this, you've talked to all the people in the bank, and they've decided they're not upset with what happened that day. The bank manager is giving you a vote of confidence in being able to reform them. That's a lot of faith in you. Do you think you'll be able to do that?" Bret raised his hand, and the judge looked at him. "You have something to add to this, young man?"

"I do, sir. When we was in there robbing the bank, Mrs. Remy here told me that she'd make sure our families were taken care of if we trusted her enough to put our guns down. It was one of the hardest decisions I ever had to make. Not putting down my gun, but giving up a chance to put a little bit of food on the table for the first time in weeks. Also, a gallon of milk in the icebox. Times are hard for everybody, sir, worse yet for ex-cons." Bret looked at her as he continued. "Not only did she not back out of her promise, but she made sure my family is in a better home. They don't have to play out in the yard where rats as big as them and snakes chase them no more. Even my brother has a better home for his own family. Sir, if this woman said she'd be able to make it work for us, I'm going to do everything in my power to make sure I follow her to the ends of the earth. There ain't none better than Mr. and Mrs. Remy."

Lizzy wanted to hug Bret. He'd been the hardest to convince that she would do her damndest to get him into this new program she was working on. When the judge asked her what she was planning for the two men, she was happy to tell him.

"This will be something for others like Mr. Rogers to benefit from. We have a decked-out bus that is a moving pantry. Anyone that needs it will be able to shop from the bus. Bret will be able to drive the bus for us, and Jefferson is going to work back at the stationary pantry to help load shelves, as well as clean up after the meals we'll be serving once we get it up and running." She asked to come forward and handed him the signed contract from each of the men on how they were going to repay the county for what they'd done. "Their wives are working too, but with an income. Fifty percent of what Bret and Jefferson are making will be paid to the county on whatever fine you give them. I will take full responsibility for their actions while they're working to make them better citizens in this town."

He asked her about other prisoners, and she was able to tell him how they now had employed ten other ex-cons, all working out well. Even Davy came forward and said that he'd been by the place a few times, and everyone was working. He also said that Mr. Dalton, a decorated police officer, and his wife, Kelly Dalton, an FBI agent, were a part of the program.

"Sounds to me like you have more back up than I do when I'm out and about." The courtroom laughed, and so did the judge. He looked at Bret and Jefferson. "Do you understand what gift you're getting here today? How this woman and her family are going to give you something that no one else would have even thought about?"

"Yes, sir. We think about that every day." Jefferson looked at his little family, then back at Winston. "Your Honor, I'll get to see my kids play without being terrified that they're going to be hurt by some wild bullet. I no longer worry if I'm going to find them frozen in their beds on account of the heat not being enough to fight with the wind blowing through the broken windows. They're safe, and that's all a person can ask for when they love theirs like me and my brother do."

"All right. I'm going to grant you this, Mrs. Remy. But I'll be watching you too. You make this work, and you surely could slow down the number of people I see in here every day. I'd like that myself." She thanked him. "Don't you be screwing this up. I know you won't, but if you need help with anything, don't you dare be afraid of asking for it. You got some good people behind you; you would be better off asking for help before you get in over your head."

"I'm well aware of how much I need all these people, sir. You included."

Winston nodded and banged his gavel on the desk. Once he said the next case should be brought up, she was engulfed in hugs by Belinda and Wilma, the wives of Bret and Jefferson.

"Does this mean Jefferson will be coming home?" Lizzy told her it did. "Oh my goodness, we're going to have to get on home and cook some dinner. You'll come, won't you? To have him home again is going to be wonderful. Just to know he's close. And the house? Why, he's going to love it as much as I do. Yes, I have to get home and get to cooking dinner. Come on, Wilma. We have a feast to cook."

She was out the door and into her car before Lizzy could tell her they'd be there for dinner. When Remy hugged her, telling her how proud of her he was, she felt good too. It was going to work, damn it. All of it was going to be working toward helping a great many people.

On the way home, they stopped and picked up some

roses for the wives. It was going to be a couple of days before they began work, and she was so happy with the outcome. Lizzy knew they'd stay on track too.

One of the things she knew the men weren't going to be able to have was alcohol, as well as firearms, which they both promised her they'd never have in the house. It was going to be hard this first couple of weeks when they started working. However, she had all the confidence in the world that it was going to work.

Chapter 10

CJ stretched out on the lawn chair and looked up at the sky. It would be snowing before morning, and she, for one, was looking forward to the cold that would end things for a while—bugs and the like. Smiling, she stood up and felt the snap of the cold touch her skin. The way the breeze blew through her hair, making it feel colder when it touched her skin again. Once she made her way into the house, she gathered up the things to make some brewed tea. She'd not had any in so long her mouth was watering for a little sip.

"I heard you come in. Have you had enough sunshine today?" Circe Jane Montgomery told her sister, Pfeiffer, that she'd never have enough sunshine. "The rest of us in the world are scrambling for something warmer, and you're outside without a coat. Or shoes, for that matter."

"I love the cold." That was an understatement. CJ couldn't think of a word that would say how much she loved the cold. "I was thinking of having a nice cup of apple tea. Would you like a cup?"

"I would love one. Also, I baked apple scones yesterday." She told her sister that was more than likely the reason she'd been craving it. "Could be. Before I forget to tell you yet again, there is a schedule opening at the store in the morning for you if you'd like to pick it up."

"I would love to pick it up." She would love to go to work tomorrow. That would leave her the rest of the day to do her other job. The one that paid their bills and made sure they had money in the bank. Working was one of the many ways she helped her big sister. "Are you and the girls going to be working on cookies tomorrow? I know they are planning the entire day around being with you."

"They've told me. I don't know how much energy I'll have for it, but I'm going to spend the day with them." Pfeiffer wasn't just her big sister, but she was her much older one. There was almost twenty years difference in their ages. Pfeiffer's daughters, Sally and Rachel, were about the same age as CJ. "I saw that you picked up the ingredients for snickerdoodles. Don't you like any other cookie than that?"

"I *can* eat other cookies, but I don't like them as much as I do those. Sally makes them just right, just enough cinnamon to sugar all over them." Both her nieces could cook and bake like their mom. CJ was lucky if she could brew a pot of tea without forgetting about the water until it was all gone. Twice that had happened to her. "When is Rachel coming home?"

"Tonight sometime. She said she was going to drive straight through. I begged her not to, but she's as stubborn as you are." That, she was sure, her sister didn't think of as a compliment. "Then we're all going to get up early and go out for breakfast."

CJ would join them in their baking if she was off, but she didn't enjoy herself. She did love them all, but they were mother and daughters, and having her there made them have to divide their time with her too. She wanted them to spend time with their mother. CJ would if she still had hers around.

Sipping her tea with her sister, they talked about the cookies they were going to bake. The three of them could have several hundred dozen cookies baked in two days and not eat a single one of them. CJ would be sick after eating a lot of cookie dough and then trying any cookie that came out of the oven. Her weakness was sweets. But her biggest was snickerdoodles.

At six, they both sat in the living room to watch the news. Dinner was over, they'd cleaned up the kitchen, and now this was the time they settled into the couch. CJ didn't much care for sitting idle, so she would work on her laptop to get a fresh start for the morning.

The house belonged to her sister now, so she set the rules for the television. Before that, their mother had owned it. Mom had left the house to the two of them. When things got to the point where Pfeiffer needed to take a loan out for college for Sally, Pfeiffer bought her out so she could use the house as collateral. CJ never bothered having it transferred back into her name. It wasn't something she was worried about.

When the news was over, they watched a couple of game shows. It was a nightly thing they both had been doing before their mom passed away. It was also their time to talk about what was going on around town, which Pfeiffer knew the most about.

"Did I tell you that Mr. Rogers got off with no fine and no jail time?" CJ loved that old man and would have taken him to see his wife had she known. "There is a new program getting started to help people out that don't have much in the way of food or transportation. I hope it works out. There are a lot of people out there that need help most of the time."

They had too before she got a good job. Like when a big bill came due at the same time as the taxes. It didn't happen as much as it used to, not with them simply not using the credit cards to pay for things. Borrowing from a credit card company to pay the electric bill or whatever was coming due had nearly made them lose their home.

They were doing all right now. Sally had graduated from college to be a teacher at the same time CJ had. Rachel was in her last year. As soon as Rachel graduated, she'd get a good job as a nurse and be able to pave her own life.

"I heard from the bank again today." CJ asked her what he had wanted. "Other than for me to go out with him, he wanted to know if we wanted to refinance this house. I have no idea why we'd want to refinance a house that we own. I told him no again and no to the dating thing too. I'm not ready for that."

"Not that I think you should date Daniel Benson, but you really should be dating again." Pfeiffer just looked at her. "Okay, we both should be dating, but it's been almost ten years. Aren't you ready to get your body waxed up for some sex starved man?"

"He would have to be sex starved to want to sleep with me." CJ told her sister they didn't usually do much sleeping when they were sex starved. "Very funny. When are you going to date again? I think it's been longer than I have since you went out on a— Oh, CJ, I'm so sorry."

"It's all right." She looked away so her sister wouldn't see the hurt. "It's been a while, I know that. But he hurt me, and I'm afraid. It took me four years to learn it wasn't my fault, even though he blamed me, and to say that he hurt me. I think it was money well spent."

They didn't speak for a few minutes, and she was all right with that. She and her sister could go days without really talking about anything serious, and it never really bothered either of them. Sometimes the quiet was better than emptying out one's brains, as her grannie said.

"I was just thinking of Grannie myself." Pfeiffer was like that. She could latch onto whatever a person was thinking without a second thought. "When was the last time you saw her? I've not been in about a week. She doesn't like me as much as she does you anyway."

"She loves you. And the girls. I went to see her just this morning on my way back from my run. Grannie still asks me why I run if there isn't anyone chasing me. But we had a nice talk. And she and I had breakfast together." Pfeiffer asked her if that was her second or third breakfast this morning. "I do believe it was only my second this time. Anyway, she was telling me about this blanket I should make. I don't know where she comes up with this idea that I can quilt, but she always has a rough draft of a pattern when she thinks of one."

"You look so much like Mom, maybe that's it. Mom loved to quilt. She wasn't as good as Grannie, but we stay warm all winter with her quilting. Well, most of us do. Do you have any more than a sheet on your bed in the winter months?" CJ told her she had one quilt on her bed. "Small wonder. I remember Dad being like you are, overheated all the time. However, I don't think I ever saw him walking around in the snow without shoes on. It's a miracle you have any feeling in your feet at all."

"I have lots of feelings in my feet, thank you very much." They both laughed, and CJ asked her why she'd brought up Grannie. "I was just thinking about how she would always have some saying about something you were doing. Like emptying your brains out."

"Yes, she did at that. I remember thinking she was nuts when I was a kid. She'd say something like that and then just walk away like I was supposed to be able to decipher whatever the heck she was talking about. My least favorite one was, 'Bachelor's wives and maid's children are well taught.' That is a contradiction all the way around."

"Of course, it is. I know the meaning. Do you want me to explain it to you?" Pfeiffer looked at her oddly, and CJ smiled. "I promise you I know what it means. It means that a childless man and a childless woman have no knowledge about maintaining a good idea about things they don't have. You see? They have these opinions about child-rearing that are wrong because they have nothing to base it on."

"Okay, that does make it sound right. What other tidbits of information do you have about her sayings? Let me think of one."

While her sister thought about what Grannie used to say, CJ read over the email that had just entered her box. It was from her boss. As her emails were coded, she put in the password to open it up.

"Something wrong?"

"I'm not sure. I have this email about the last job I did. He's saying he didn't get it. However, not only does it have the work order number on it that I assigned, but the attachment is attached to the reply he sent." Pfeiffer asked her if that made better sense in her head. "Yes. What I mean is, I attached the job to an email that he just replied to me on. On it is the attached job. It's been opened too. The email and the attachment."

"How do you know he opened them?" She said her email told her that. "You can fix it so you know if someone opens your email? I'd like to have that on mine. I have people telling me all the time they didn't get their bill."

"I'll fix it for you in the morning. Not only will it tell you if someone opened it, but also which computer it was opened on. Like you'd know it was me that opened it because of the IP address that's there." She looked at her sister's expression. "You have no idea what I'm talking about, do you? How can you live here with me and not have a clue what I'm going on about most of the time?"

"Because you're brilliant, and I'm just a homebody that loves you to pieces?" CJ hugged her as she dug into the popcorn bowl. "As for Grannie, I'm not sure I will ever figure her out. She's a great deal like you in all ways. I think I remember her being warm all the time too. Must have skipped me. Thankfully." CJ laughed.

They watched television until ten, then CJ went up to her room. She didn't go to bed, but worked from her computer for a while before she'd lay down. Never being one that needed a full eight hours of sleep, CJ could sleep for an hour or two before getting up fresh as a daisy.

Not her sister or nieces. If they didn't get at least eight or nine hours, they were crabby all day. And she'd never get in the way of their first cup of coffee. CJ didn't have vices like that to get her going. She could even skip eating a meal sometimes.

Her phone ringing woke her from a dead sleep. It took her only seconds to realize the person on the other end of the phone had the wrong number. She asked him to slow down and say what he needed once more.

"I've found a woman on the side of the road." Okay, CJ sat up in her bed, pulling on clothing as he continued. "She's been hurt badly, and I'm helping her along. The last number she called was this one. I don't know her name, but I was wondering if you could meet me at the hospital."

"Where are you?" He told her which road he was on and the mile marker. "Okay. You said the woman had been beaten up. Can you tell me what she looks like?"

Instead of answering her, she got a picture of the woman. It was her niece Rachel, and she did look really bad. Her mind skittered over his comment that he was helping her along, and she refused to think he was helping her along by hurting her more. CJ grabbed her keys and was out the door before she spoke again.

"I'm on my way. The hospital closest to you is Mercy. Can you get her there?" He said he was standing outside their emergency room doors now. "What are you? Who are you?"

"My name is Brian. Vampire. Are you going to have a hissy fit now about this?" She asked him if that was the usual reaction he got when he saved someone's life. "Yes. Vampires have a bad rep."

"So long as you're helping my niece, I'm all right with you being whatever you need to be. I'm leaving my house now. I'm not telling her mom until I'm positive it's her." Brian asked her if she was usually so cautious. "You have no idea."

It was the longest drive of her life. Twenty minutes cut down to fifteen wasn't bad, but she wanted to get there in one piece. As soon as she walked into the ER, she stopped at the desk. Whatever was going on, CJ had a feeling that somehow it was her fault.

~*~

Brian watched the two women. CJ had called her sister when Rachel was taken to surgery. Her voice was calm, and even though she'd not shared the information with him, he knew that CJ was blaming herself for her niece being hurt. Pfeiffer, he assumed when they hugged, came in just as he was going to try and leave them to their family. The much younger woman hugged her as well. He knew they were all related by the way they looked like clones of one another.

"Don't leave." He shook his head at CJ and said he couldn't add anymore than he already had to the police. "I understand. You did save her life. You have no idea how much that means to all of us."

He could have told her more than he had the police. Brian could have told her that he had the scent of the two men that had beaten the young lady. The place where her car had been run off the road, and the woman trying to get away from them. However, he didn't. Being involved at all was something he didn't feel comfortable about. But when he got to Bancroft's, he was going to tell him everything, including who the men were and how he'd killed them both. There was evidence, too, that they had *thought* they had the woman in front of him. CJ was wanted by a lot of unsavory people.

"I just happened to be in the right place at the right time." She pointed to her lip and said he had a little spot on him. Licking away the drop of blood, he smiled at her. "You're taking this very well for not knowing about my kind."

"I know a great deal about your kind. I don't believe I've ever met a vampire before, but...." When she looked around, he did as well. But instead of talking to him about it, she pulled him into the ladies' room. After checking each stall, she locked the door. "Do you happen to know a person by the name of Bancroft? I'm not sure if that's his last or first name. Wait, don't answer that. I doubt you were going to anyway, but don't answer. If you happen to come across him at any point soon, you should tell him a task force is being put together that is hoping to kill him off."

"Do you happen to know why? I mean, if I ever run across him in my lifetime, he might well ask me the same question." She nodded. This time she put out her hand and put a thumb drive into his palm as they shook hands. He nodded. "You just happened to have this on you in the event you found a vampire?"

"No. I have that on me all the time. If it were to fall into the wrong hands, I wouldn't be found." Brian wondered what was on the drive and why she trusted him with it. "I can see you have thousands of questions. I do, as well. However, I can tell you this much here. I work for different companies by putting security systems in place. Firewalls if they want them. Sometimes it's only putting in a program that gets employees to clock in and out. With that, I can walk around in their brains, the ones on their computer. I came across that three days ago when I was working for an office."

"And you trust me with this, why?" She told him she had no idea why, but she *did* trust him. "I have your scent now, CJ. If you're trying to fuck me over, I'll hunt you down and kill you."

"All right." She put out her hand again. "Would you please have a connection to me? I know how that works. You'll be in my head all the time. I would like that, so if I am in trouble or I find out something more, I can give you fair warning. Also, if I'm taken, which I think will happen daily, then perhaps you can save me as well."

"Again, I don't understand this. For whatever reason, I have the same sort of trust with you." She nodded and stood there. "All right, CJ, I'll take your blood, but you must take mine as well. That will give us a tighter connection so that I will also know where you are if you're taken."

"I'm all right with that. However, if it comes to a choice for you to save me or my family, they're to be at the top of your list. I won't have anything happen to them because I'm good with computers." He said he would do that for her. "Promise me, Brian. I can't stand the thought of someone harming them. But they will, to get to me.

Promise me."

"I promise that if there is a time I can either save you or your family, I will save them." He grinned, not even bothering to hide his fangs. "However, I will do my damndest to make sure you're safe as well."

She left the bathroom before he did after they exchanged blood drops. Pulling shadows around him, he waited until someone came in and left when the door was still open. Brian didn't know what to do now. If he stayed here, CJ and her family would be safe. If he went to talk to Bancroft, he'd be able to figure out what was going on with the drive. Smiling to himself, he thought of the perfect plan.

Hello, Bancroft. I'm in serious need of you to send someone here to Mercy Hospital. I have something for you. He asked him why he couldn't come. *I don't know precisely, but your name has come up attached to someone wanting to kill you.*

I see. Do you happen to know who this person is? He explained to his oldest and dearest friend what had happened in the last few hours. *Okay. This woman, do you know her name? Anything about her?*

Her name is Circe Jane Montgomery. She goes by CJ. I do know that she works on computers. However, we have exchanged blood, and she is someone that I instinctively trust. I have no idea why, but I know she's not lying to me and that she's scared of being killed. Bancroft told him that Kelly wanted to go get whatever it was he had. *Thumb drive. And make sure Kelly isn't alone. I don't know what's on this drive, but they might have some knowledge of her as well.*

Brian, you're scaring me a little. He told him he was sorry, but he thought this was important. *I agree with you, but it doesn't make me any less afraid. I'm an old vampire, and to think that someone out there thinks they can kill me makes me wonder what sort of lengths they're willing to go to.*

By the time Kelly and Donald showed up, Rachel was out of surgery and in recovery. The other women were with her. CJ told him she was going to make a full recovery, but it was going to be a long road.

"I have someone that is going to take the drive with them. I'm going to stay here to make sure the four of you are safe. I don't know who might be coming to get you, but you're vulnerable here. Too many people coming and going all the time."

"Thank you." She didn't say anything for a few seconds, and he decided this woman knew a great deal more than she was letting on. *I was just thinking about something. Something that I got back from one of my clients last night. He said he didn't get the program I sent him. However, it was opened, as was the email. I wonder if his computer has been compromised. It can't be mine. I'm too good to let that happen. But what if someone is trying to get to me through some of the people I work for? Then, in turn to Bancroft?*

I know squat about computers at the level you seem to have. But I'd say if they were trying to get to Bancroft — who I do know, by the way — then they'd do whatever they can to make you a target. She told him that was what she was just thinking. *I* know you love your family, CJ, but you shouldn't stay around them. The farther you are away from them, the safer they can be. Also, I'm going to send someone to your home when your family leaves.

My Grannie. I forgot about her. Can you make sure she's safe as well? He said he would. CJ told him where she was and the code word to give to her if she had to leave with someone other than her. *I've left nothing to chance, I thought, but right now, I feel my life unraveling at a high rate of speed.*

I'm going to do my best at keeping you all safe. Even Bancroft will if it comes to that. Can you tell me, through our link, what is the reason they want to kill my friend? She was thinking. It was tempting to look into her mind to see what all she knew, but he also knew to do that would put a wedge between them and their trust for each other. *You don't have to if you don't think —*

Bancroft is a lord of a kiss. I'm not sure what that is. A kiss I understand, but not what him being a lord is. Several hundred years ago, Bancroft purchased a large chunk of land that is now worth billions. His wife is human and corrupted. Their words, not mine. Their plan is to kill him and take his wife. I know that doesn't sound like much of a reason to kill him, but that's only one part of the information on the drive. That drive holds information about six different companies and their mentioning of Bancroft. He asked if that was the worst. *Not even close. They want to take him to a lab and drain his blood to give to the highest bidder. They believe by draining him and selling his blood, they'll have humans all over the world wanting some of it to live forever. I'm not sure, but I don't think that'll work. But then, that's one of the other plots. The worst one I came across was a satanic group that wishes to use him to call forth the devil, so they can be one with their god.*

Christ. CJ told him that she thought so as well. *All right. I've given the drive to Kelly, and Donald, the man that came with her, is going to pop her home. I'm not leaving here until you decide what you wish to do.*

I guess you're right. I have to leave. He said he was sorry. *As am I. They're all I have, and I don't want to leave them.*

He didn't tell her it might not do any good to leave them. If they knew about her family, they'd used them no matter where she was. Thinking along those lines, he thought he was going to need more help than he'd first thought. They needed to just disappear, the entire family.

He looked at Kelly when she sat down next to him. Telling her everything through the link they had because of her being mated to Bancroft, he also told her what he wanted to do. Hide them. All of them.

All right. Let me make a couple of calls, not to my work. As yet, we don't know how these people are affiliated with other people. We can put them in our home, and they'd be safe for a while, but I think they need to be hidden deeper than that. Brian thanked her for going to so much trouble for him. *You would have done the same for us.*

Yes. Without a second thought. She smiled at him, and he felt his face heat with *embarrassment. I walked right into that one, didn't I?*

I won't hold it against you. But I'm glad to know that, even though we've only just met, you'd take care of me. Okay. You and Donald stay here, and I'll see what I can do from home. For now, we'll just have them as guests at our home. I think that it will be safer than at their home. By the way, did you kill the men that beat up her sister?

Yes. She said she thought so. They'd found their bodies an hour ago. *I was pissed off that they'd hurt someone. They really did a number on her too. Without my blood, she would have surely died before I could get her to the hospital.*

I'm assuming neither of them are your mate. He explained to her the feelings he had concerning CJ. *Is that something important? What I mean is, is she one of the others' mates? I'm still learning things here.*

I never thought of that, but she could very well be. He thought of how the other vampires he knew were protective of women. *It could also be that we've been ingrained with the need to protect all females. I know I was sort of beaten over the head with how to protect the women of any species. We can test that theory when Donald gets back.*

It certainly would make her safer if she was one of their mates. She stood up and hugged him. *Donald is going to pop me home, then come back. I'll let you know what we find on the drive. We're going to only open it with a laptop without any access to other computers. Perhaps we should send someone to their home to clean it out.*

Good idea. She hugged him again, and Donald appeared behind her. *Don't forget to let me know. I like this woman, and*

I don't want anything to happen to her family. I've sent someone after Grannie too.

After Kelly left and Donald returned, the two of them sat in the lobby of the ER and watched people. It was somewhat fun. They made up a game together where they would guess why they were there before looking. CJ reached out to him to let him know that her niece was in her room now. After getting that from her, Donald and he walked up the stairs to the second floor and waited for them there. In less time than he thought it should have taken them, the Montgomery family was sitting with them. Looking over at Donald, he asked him what was wrong.

Nothing. He asked him a second time but asked if one of the women was his mate. *Yes. I'm thinking it's the one walking around. But they're all so close together I'm having a hard time figuring it out. They smell the same.*

I'd not mention that if I were you. I don't know how a woman's mind works, but if you tell her she smells like other women, I'm sure you might lose your head. He nodded but kept watching the four of them. *This is good, right? I mean, whatever one you are mated to, you can be happy in knowing that they're all right as humans.*

Laugh it up, Brian. This only means you might be next.

Teasing his friend was fun. Brian thought he might be the only one to welcome a mate into his heart. He was looking forward to it more than he had anything for a long time.

Convincing the women wasn't nearly as difficult as

they thought it would be. They knew that CJ wouldn't have told them it was dangerous if it wasn't. The fact that one of them had been hurt badly helped to persuade them as well. Taking them home one at a time, CJ and Rachel were the last to leave. It was then that Donald knew which one was his mate. He didn't know which one of them was taking it harder, either.

Before You Go...

HELP AN AUTHOR

write a review

THANK YOU!

Share your voice and help guide other readers to these wonderful books. Even if it's only a line or two, your reviews help readers discover the author's books so they can continue creating stories that you'll love. Log in to your favorite retailer and leave a review. Thank you.

AWARD WINNING, BESTSELLING AUTHOR

Kathi Barton, a winner of the Pinnacle Book Achievement award as well as a best-selling author on Amazon and All Romance books, lives in Nashport, Ohio, with her husband, Paul. When not creating new worlds and romance, Kathi and her husband enjoy camping and going to auctions. She can also be seen at county fairs with her husband, who is an artist and potter.

Her muse, a cross between Jimmy Stewart and Hugh Jackman, brings her stories to life for her readers in a way that has them coming back time and again for more. Her favorite genre is paranormal romance, with a great deal of spice. You can visit Kathi on line and drop her an email if you'd like. She loves hearing from her fans. aaronskiss@gmail.com.

Follow Kathi on her blog: http://kathisbartonauthor.blogspot.com/